The American Girl Book of HORSE STORIES

Selected by the Editors of
The American Girl Magazine

Illustrated by Sam Savitt

A WINDWARD BOOK

Random House  *New York*

Windward Books are published by Random House, Inc.
First Windward Silverback Edition, October 1972.
Originally published by Random House, Inc., in 1963.

Library of Congress catalog card number: 63-18285

ISBN: 0-394-82192-0

Contents

The American Girl Book of Horse Stories

Margaret Leighton

Danger Rides the River Road

Robin's hoofs beat a drumming tattoo on the frozen turf of the meadow. Faster, faster! Vinnie leaned forward, gathering the reins on his neck. "Up, boy!" she cried. The big chestnut cleared the high rail fence superbly, with hardly a break in his stride.

"Sure-footed as a cat, I vow and declare!" she told herself. "There won't be a better-mounted dragoon in the troop than our Nat!"

For Vinnie was riding her soldier-brother's horse. He had cared for Robin as a colt, but the animal had been too young to ride when Nat had joined General Washington's courageous little army. Now that army was encamped on the Hudson, doggedly holding the newly formed nation together against the British threat to split it apart at the river. Any day might bring news of battle echoing northward into this quiet New England countryside.

"He has the bones and legs of a jumper," Nat had said on his last morning at home. "If he were only a year older, what a mount I would have!"

"I'll train him to jump for you," Vinnie had offered, her eyes wide and earnest. "I'll have him ready for you this time next year."

"You?" Nat had laughed and pulled one of the brown curls that escaped from under her fluted muslin cap. "A young female on a jumper? What would Aunt Hortense say to that?"

"Aunt Hortense!" Vinnie echoed heatedly. " 'Lavinia, get on with your spinning. Lavinia, mind your manners. Lavinia, rip out this whole seam and sew it again properly.' Oh, we were happy enough before she came here to live with us, just you and Grandfather and me!"

"Someone had to teach a small hoyden how to become a young lady." Nat had laughed again.

"But don't worry about me, sweetheart. Grandfather has given me Admiral—a good-enough horse, though no match for what this fellow will be someday."

But when Nat rode away, young and straight in the saddle, Vinnie hadn't forgotten. Hardly a day passed in the months which followed that she did not have Robin out, no matter what the weather. In this she had her grandfather for an ally against Aunt Hortense's horrified protests.

Even when she donned a pair of Nat's outgrown doeskin breeches, the old man had silenced his daughter gruffly. "Let the lass alone. Who else is there on the place who can ride to fences? Not you, nor I, nor old Jabez. The best I can do is fire off my pistol and season the beast to gunpowder. A dragoon's horse can't be trained in petticoats!"

Now Vinnie had circled Robin about to head for the fence again when she saw a figure hurrying toward her through the orchard of leafless apple trees. Beyond, past the barns and sheds, the brick house among its dormant gardens stood enthroned on a little eminence above the bare fields that sloped down to the horseshoe curve of the river. It was Patty, the stout young housemaid, her full skirts and white apron billowing about her and her cap ribbons streaming.

"Miss Lavinia!" she called above the wind. "Miss Vinnie!"

Vinnie guided Robin to her and drew rein. "What is it, Patty?" she asked.

"Mrs. Hortense sent me to fetch you in," Patty said. "The parson's expected for tea and she wants you to get out of"—she broke into a giggle—"them disgraceful pantaloons and into your sprigged muslin in time to pour the tea. And she sent me to the storeroom for a mug of lavender water, too. She said you'd need it to get the smell of horse off you."

Vinnie was shaping a saucy answer when she heard her name called from another quarter. She turned in her saddle. Ten-year-old Benjy Sawyer, son of their nearest neighbor, was running toward them across the frosty stubble field. His cheeks were red, his eyes wide.

"Something's wrong at the Sawyers'," Vinnie cried. "What is it, Benjy? What's happened?" She spurred to meet him.

"It's the British!" Benjy shouted, "Ma sent me across the field to warn you. There's British troopers coming by the river road!"

Patty clapped her hand to her mouth. "British! Lawk-a-mercy, they'll cut our throats for sure!"

"British!" Vinnie echoed, feeling her heart bound with quick fear. What could bring them so far into this hostile countryside if not to try to capture her grandfather, a well-known and prominent patriot? Praise heaven, he was away, gone on a journey that would take him several days.

"It's horses they're after," Benjy was explaining breathlessly. "They've taken both the saddle mares from Colby's farm already and others from down river. They're paying the Tories but not the patriots."

Horses? This was different. Grandfather had his own and his manservant's mount with him. Only Toby, the good old plowhorse, was in the barnyard. *And Robin!*

Vinnie's first thought was to gallop straight for the woods and hide there. But to reach them she must cross not only all the open fields, but also the road by which the troopers were coming. She was still shielded from sight by the thin fringe of fruit trees, but she was fairly trapped. If they had passed the Sawyers' already, they would be upon her at any moment.

"They *shan't* take Nat's horse!" she cried.

Could they pile hay over Robin and conceal him in one of the sheds? No, even if there were time for that it would be useless. The barn and sheds would be the first places raiders would search. But—a wild thought raced through her mind—the last place they would search would be—

No time now to weigh the chances. Vinnie spurred Robin forward, leaving Ben and Patty open-mouthed. Over the box hedge, across the lawn and bare flower beds, she rode the big chestnut, and pulled him to a clattering halt on the brick terrace that ran along the back of the house. Dismounting, she flung open the door into the rear of the wide central hall. "Come on, boy—gently, gently—" she urged him, pulling on the reins.

But after one terrified look through the unfamiliar, narrow opening, Robin would not budge. He planted his feet and hauled back on the bit. When Vinnie tugged harder he flung up his head and almost jerked the reins from her hands.

"Come on, old fellow. Oh, please, please!" She pulled again, and this time Robin reared high, ears back, eyes rolling.

Patty and Ben had now joined her. Patty wrung her hands and flapped her apron ineffec-

tually, while Benjy slapped at Robin's flanks with his hat and was nearly kicked for his pains. He moved farther off, then gave a shout of alarm. "Here they come! I can see their red coats through the willows. Look, there, where the road leaves the river to cross your land! It's too late now."

"No!" A memory had flashed into Vinnie's mind. She snatched Patty's apron off, rolled it swiftly, and tied it over Robin's eyes. "That's what Jabez did when the barn took fire and the horses wouldn't come out. Now Robin, dear Robin, come along. Soo-oo, boy."

Blindfolded, Robin became suddenly docile. He allowed himself to be led through the door into the hall, where he stood shifting his hooves uneasily on the polished floor. His nostrils flared as he drew nervous breaths in and out, sniffing the unfamiliar indoor smells and trembling spasmodically. But he was inside, and the door was shut behind him.

"Lavinia!" Aunt Hortense's voice was a prolonged, shrill shriek as she swept down the stairs, the maroon silk of her gown rustling and the lace-trimmed cap on top of her powdered hair fairly quivering with indignation. "Lavinia, truly this is the last straw. Take that creature out of here this instant!"

"But Aunt, there's no other place to hide him. There are British troopers on the road—Benjy brought word. They're after horses and I won't let them have Nat's Robin."

"British!" Mrs. Hortense shrieked again, but more faintly. She paled and clutched at the newel. "British?"

"You can see them yourself on the river road, ma'am," Patty said. She had opened the door at the opposite end of the hall and was shading her eyes with her hand. "Redcoats, for sure."

"Shut that door and bolt it!" Vinnie cried.

"But they're soldiers with guns and swords." Patty's eyes were filled with terror. "They'll cut all our throats if we anger them, I tell you."

"And if they come to the door there, they can see plain as day through those glass panes on both sides, right here into the back of the hall," Ben pointed out practically.

"It's no use, my poor child," Aunt Hortense said. "Don't be foolish. We must be thankful, at least, that your grandfather is away."

"I will *not* let them have Robin," Vinnie declared desperately, and even while she was saying it another idea came to her. "Help me, Ben." She was pulling the nervous, edgy animal toward another door.

With a swirl of skirts Aunt Hortense swept past her to bar the way. "Not in there. Never will I allow that animal in my own parlor!"

"They've stopped at the gate," Patty cried from her post. "There's an officer and five—no, six men. They're leading near twenty horses already."

Ben ran to join her at the leaded panes beside the door. "There's old Tory Soames with them. He's the one who has been telling them where the best horses are."

"Henry Soames?" The color flared into Aunt Hortense's thin cheeks. "Is that villain behind this?"

"He has seen Robin. He knows how good he is," Vinnie moaned. "Oh, *please* let me hide him in your parlor, Aunt. It's our only chance."

"Very well." Aunt Hortense stepped aside and opened the door herself. "But I shall stay in here with him and make sure he does no harm. Benjamin, you come with me. As for you, Lavinia, I leave it to you to confront them, Miss. I've never told an untruth yet and I shan't begin now. I'll not perjure my soul for any four-legged beast."

Robin was no sooner inside the little back parlor, Aunt Hortense's own special domain, than Vinnie flew up the stairs. No time to change her clothes. She tugged off the spurred boots, pulled her quilted petticoat and sprigged-muslin frock on over the riding breeches, pushed her wind-blown hair under a fresh cap, and stepped into her silver-buckled shoes.

Patty, unwilling to be left alone, had followed her and now stood peering through the starched bedroom curtains. "Oh, they're evil-looking wretches, to be sure, in their lobster-red coats. They've left two soldiers down on the road holding the string of horses. The officer and Tory Soames are coming here to the house, but the soldiers are making straight for the barn. There's old Jabez hobbling out to meet them."

"They'll get no help from him, at least," Vinnie said thankfully. "How he hates a redcoat! He'll pretend he's too deaf to understand what they want. There, I'm ready. This dress is woefully tight without my stays. Fasten the back for me, please, Patty."

Lavinia felt Patty's icy hands pull the edges of

her dress together. Just as she finished both girls froze to silence, for the sound of the door knocker echoed hollowly through the house. Patty opened the door and scuttled back to take refuge with Mrs. Hortense in the back parlor. Vinnie held her ground, although she felt her knees quaking under the sprigged muslin. The opened door revealed a young officer in the hated British scarlet and beside him Henry Soames, stocky and heavy-jowled. Henry's beady eyes peered into the shadowed depths of the hall.

"Is your grandfather home?" he asked.

Vinnie turned pointedly away from him and addressed the officer. "What is your business here, sir?" she asked. "There are no menfolk at home, only my aunt and myself and the servants. Please go away."

The young lieutenant touched his goldlaced hat courteously. "Be assured, Miss, you've nothing to fear from us. I've come on His Majesty's business to secure horses in the King's name for the King's troops."

"We have no horses here for the King," Lavinia answered, and she felt her heart race under her tight bodice.

"I told you they were stubborn rebels. The old rogue's a neighborhood ringleader," Soames muttered. "But they *have* four good horses, as I said."

"We have no horses for King George," Lavinia repeated, more firmly this time, anger at Soames bringing her courage back.

The officer frowned. "I must do my duty, Miss. I'll have the horses, whether or no, and your saucy tongue has lost you the chance to be paid for them."

"The only horse you'll find in our stables today is a twelve-year-old plow horse," Lavinia told him. "Most of our farm work is done by oxen. Ask the stableman, he'll tell you. My grandfather has his riding horses with him, I'm glad to say."

Soames gave an angry snort. "The wench is lying. The thoroughbred I told you of is here, at least. I saw a stableboy putting him over that gate not an hour ago."

At the word "stableboy" Lavinia heard Patty's startled giggle from the parlor.

"Lieutenant," Vinnie said quickly, "this man is only trying to pay off a grudge. He has brought you here for nothing. We haven't had a stableboy for months, only old Jabez, who couldn't mount a horse to save his soul."

While the officer stood looking indecisively from glowering man to angry girl, a trooper appeared and saluted stiffly.

"Sir, there are no horses here at all, save an old nag in the barnyard that wouldn't be worth the skinning," he reported. "We've searched all the buildings and, as you can see, the pastures and fields are as bare as the palm of my hand."

The lieutenant turned on Soames. "What have you to say to that? Who's lying now?"

Soames's face was purple. "The horse *must* be here. I tell you I saw it myself. A big chestnut. They've hidden it somewhere."

"Bah! Try to hide a horse! You've led us six miles out of our way for nothing, when every hour counts. If we have a rebel patrol cutting us off before we get back to our lines, you'll be to blame." He was turning away when a noise from inside the house halted him. It was a tremendous, thudding clatter, followed by a crash and a woman's scream. Paralyzed with horror, Vinnie could only stand wide-eyed and rigid.

The lieutenant looked startled. "Pink my soul!

The roof must be falling in," he said. "Is anyone hurt?"

"I'll just go in and have a look," Soames said, and stepped quickly into the hall.

"No, no!" Vinnie caught his arm and struggled to hold him back, but it was no use. He pulled her with him along the hall and had almost reached the parlor when the door opened suddenly. Aunt Hortense emerged, still a majestic figure although her cap was wildly tilted and a jagged rip showed in her silken gown. In her hand, moreover, she held the long, brass-handled toasting fork, and it was the sharp prongs that halted the Tory in his tracks.

"Henry Soames!" she cried. "Henry Soames inside this house! Out with you, villain, rogue, scum! It's enough that a clumsy menial has upset my best china cabinet without having this house polluted by such as you. Out of here, I say!"

Soames was backing rapidly toward the door while Aunt Hortense, brandishing the fork under his nose, pressed her advantage hard. He reached the threshold, stumbled over it, and turned for help to the soldiers. But his words were cut abruptly by a leap and a cry of pain as Aunt Hortense jabbed the fork into his coattails. It did not soothe his temper to hear guffaws of laughter from the British soldiers.

"Come, Mr. Soames, get on your horse," the lieutenant called to him. "That is, if you can sit him. The lady has routed you fairly, and we've had enough of this wild-goose chase of yours. We've no more time to waste. Your servant, Madam, and yours too, Miss." He saluted smartly and clattered away down the drive. The troopers fell in, two and two behind him. Soames struggled into his saddle and trailed after them.

As they vanished from sight among the willows, Vinnie drew a deep, free breath. "Saved! Robin is saved—and by *you*, Aunt Hortense!" She flung her arms about her aunt. All the long months of smoldering resentment and dislike were dissolved in a warm rush of gratitude.

"Well!" Mrs. Hortense freed herself at last. "Nat should thank us both. But bless us all, what a sight I must be, and the parson will arrive any minute. And my parlor! Lavinia, you and Benjy remove that animal at once. It will take more than lavender water to make the room presentable, I assure you. Patty, lay the tea table in the front room and cut another plum cake. I fed the other to that horse to keep him quiet."

"Did—did Robin really knock over your china cabinet?" Lavinia asked.

"Yes, he did. But much as I valued it and its contents, I vow that one jab into Tory Soames's coattails was well worth their loss."

"Oh, Aunt Hortense," Vinnie embraced her again. "I do love you most truly!"

Mrs. Hortense submitted to this second onslaught with good grace, then drew away, straightening her cap. Her cheeks were flushed and her eyes bright. She looked pleased and almost pretty. "That's all very well, Lavinia," she said. "But I hope you will bear in mind that I let no word of untruth pass my lips. When I said 'clumsy menial,' it was very clear in my mind that the horse is man's faithful servant."

Vinnie, her eyes bright with tears and laughter, answered demurely, "Yes, Aunt Hortense."

Carolyn St. Clair King

Beautiful and Free

Gil Bronson was in the mow, forking down the last of the treasured hay to the cows that could no longer forage on the drought-browned range. When he heard the rumble of wagon wheels, he knew his father was back from town. So very soon now, Gil would know the best, or the worst, that could happen to him.

If there was someone with Dad, it would be the cattle buyer. Cattle buyers, in this hard year, were as scarce as grass, and the news that there was one in town had sent Dad off as fast as he could hitch the team. But if his father was alone, it would mean that he had had no luck. And that meant the end of Gil's long-cherished dream of going off to school in town.

He was fifteen, now, and a year had passed since his graduation from the one-room school which served their district. But going to school in the city meant boarding out, buying books and getting clothes that were different from overalls and his father's castoff, high-heeled boots. What with the drought and loss of cattle, and then no market for the steers they had saved, Dad simply had not had the cash. But if Dad sold the steers today, he had promised Gil that he could go to school.

There were no voices in the yard—just Dad saying, "So, there, Bess. Up a little, Ben." Then the rattle of loosened traces.

Gil knew the worst. But he forced his stiff legs down the ladder and even managed a frozen smile. "Hi, Dad. No luck in town, I guess."

Ben Bronson shook his grizzled head. "Young Fealy was there, in that car of his, and he took the cattle buyer off with him. Fealy's been able to feed this summer, after the range dried up, and he has a lot of beef for sale—all the buyer's going to want, I reckon. I might have saved myself the trip." He cleared a husky throat. "I did manage to buy some hay to tide us over with those cows we're feeding, Gil."

"That's good," Gil said. "I had to scrape the mow this morning." His cheeks felt stiff, and his voice was wooden. Dad buying hay—that meant he had had to use the money they had all been hoarding, a dime or a dollar at a time, in the old tin can on the kitchen shelf. There had not been enough there yet to get Gil started off to school, but it had been a nest egg, anyhow.

Ben Bronson sighed and rubbed a hand across the stubble on his chin. "I'm sorry, Gil," he said.

Gil knew that was true, and he felt ashamed to be adding trouble to the load his father had to carry.

"Sure, Dad," he said. "I've sort of given up the notion of going off to school. I'm getting kind of old for that, and besides I reckon you need me here."

His father's look of pleased relief was pretty chilly comfort, though. At dinnertime the potatoes stuck in Gil's tight throat, and he wasn't hungry.

Ben Bronson, trying for a cheerful note, broke the painful silence. "Everyone in town is agog over the wild-horse hunt tomorrow. Protheroe has offered a thousand bucks to whoever captures that outlaw stallion they call Black Prince. Five hundred dollars for his mate."

They had known about the hunt, of course. It had been organized by the wealthy rancher who had a covetous eye on the two wild creatures—the last of the bands of horses that had roamed these hills since the early days when the Spaniards had come in search of the fabled golden cities.

Gil's mother looked at him with a sudden bright and hopeful smile.

"Gil," she said, "you ought to go. You've always been crazy about that stallion. When you were younger, I couldn't keep you home from the Hesperus flats, where you could watch those two wild horses. Knowing their habits as you do, you might be the one to win that money and put yourself through a year of school."

Gil's laugh was hollow. "Gosh, Ma," he said, "the finest riders in the country will all be there. What chance do you figure old Rex would have against—well, say Jim Fealy's Scamp? That thoroughbred will leave the other bangtails standing still."

"Jim Fealy should be barred," Ma said. "All the money those Fealys have."

"No, he shouldn't," Gil protested. "Jim's entitled to his fun, just as much as anybody. Although I can't imagine its being fun. It makes me sick to think of someone's rope around Black Prince's neck. He's a beauty, sure enough, but it's something that's sort of all tied up with his running wild and being free. And the mare—you never saw her like, nor the way the two of 'em stick together. If one or the other is out of sight, they act as crazy as our old Bess with an unweaned colt."

"Protheroe aims to keep Black Prince," Ben said, "and send the mare back east to his married daughter. Just the same, Gil boy, I'd have a try at that prize. Someone's going to win it. Might as well be you."

Ben cleared his throat and left the table. Ma sat there, anxiously watching Gil, who was staring blankly into space.

It really hurt the folks, Gil knew, not being able to send him off to the school he had planned on for so many years. There really wasn't any chance of his winning the Protheroe prize—let alone the fact he could never bear to put a rope on Black Prince's neck—but if it would make the folks feel better. . . .

"All right, I'll go," he told his mother.

Gil didn't sleep well that night. He dreamed of going off to school, leading Black Prince by a fine new halter. But it wasn't a pleasant dream and when Gil woke up he wished he hadn't said he would ride in the Protheroe hunt.

As soon as breakfast was over, however, he saddled his old cow pony, Rex, and put the thick meat sandwich Ma had fixed for him inside his buttoned denim jacket. He wore scarred and scuffed old leather chaps to protect his legs if the chase should lead through heavy brush, and his father's old broad-brimmed hat.

The sun was lifting a cautious eye above the eastward peaks when Gil, completing the five-mile climb, reined his pony through the dew-drenched grass of the high flat meadow where the Protheroe hunt was now assembled.

Gil knew everybody there, except a short and bulbous man who was riding with the elder Fealy. Young Jim Fealy was there, of course, on his thoroughbred, and several other cowboys rode mounts that were notable for speed. It was just as Gil had thought it would be, and it sort of let him out, he reasoned, feeling glad deep inside. Raising his hand in silent answer to the shouted greetings, he took his place with the other riders.

Then Lou Protheroe came riding up, important on his tall, black horse, and raised a large authoritative palm.

"Now, folks," Lou said, "just a few instructions. I've had some boys out there all night keeping tabs on the two wild horses. They're grazing in a little draw, up near the head of Canyon Creek. We're going up there, and when I signal, the boys will start the outlaws down our way. When they break from cover, we'll chase 'em up across the flats toward the fence I've built across that narrow neck of land between Devil's Gulch and Big Arroyo. With you *hombres* coming up behind, we'll have 'em neatly trapped. Then it's just a question of who will be the lucky jigger to slip his noose around a thousand dollars—or half of that, if you snag the sorrel."

Protheroe's smile flashed, and the assembled cowboys yelled and waved their broad-brimmed hats.

Gil thought: I hope the Black Prince fools 'em.

And it wasn't sour grapes, either, for the closer the moment came when those two wild creatures would be imprisoned, the less Gil could bear it.

He tailed the laughing bunch up to the flat below the gulch where the outlaws grazed, pulling Rex to the farthest end as they ranged their horses in one long line.

When Protheroe raised his gun and fired, the following minutes seemed to Gil to stretch as tight as banjo wire. Every eye, along with his, strained toward the opening of the draw where the Prince and his mate would appear. And it wasn't long until Gil saw them, bursting startled from the brush.

On a grassy knoll. limned against the cobalt blue of the morning sky, they paused at sight of that line of riders.

The stallion's coat gleamed black as water under winter ice, the heavy mane floating like a dusky cloud from the high arched neck, the long black tail barely clearing the rocky ground. And by his side, just as beautiful in her way, stood the clean-limbed, round-bodied little mare, glowing embered where the sun's first rays touched her sorrel coat; her sweeping mane and fanning tail the color of a cup of well-creamed coffee.

A gasp of awe and admiration ran down the line of waiting riders. Then, like dynamited earth, suddenly and with a roar, the line burst forth in hot pursuit.

As the outlaws stood for another second, it seemed to Gil that the mare looked doubtfully toward her partner. But every line of the Prince was defiant, his head flung high and nostrils flaring, while clear above the cowboy yells and the thunder of their horses' hooves, Gil could hear his challenging trumpet call.

Black Prince dipped his nose to touch the mare's. Then the two were off like triggered bullets, leaving the scattered field of riders streaming far behind.

Gil, on his ancient horse, transfixed, incapable of motion, knew that the speed which had so often saved them would only bring them faster, now, to the fate in store for them.

And now Gil, too, spurred his pony across the flat. As he topped a little rise, he could see the race strung out ahead.

Black Prince was just a thin black streak, the mare a flash of tossing mane; and Jim Fealy on his thoroughbred was still a good half mile behind. There was no one close to Jim, and Gil knew that the Prince was already his. For when the outlaws reached the fence and, finding themselves hemmed between the two deep gulches, were forced to turn, Jim would be there with his lariat.

That was something, Gil decided, that he simply could not bear to see. On sudden impulse, he reined his mount across the rim of Big Arroyo, which was shallow here at its lower end. Having gained the sandy bottom, Gil spurred Rex up the smooth, flat floor with no other purpose in his mind than to feel the clean, cold rush of morning wind against his face and forget a little, if he could, what was happening up there on the flat.

As Gil rode up it, the arroyo deepened, till finally its eroded banks rose sheer and clifflike to the rim, and all his upward glance could find was a slice of sky with a small white cloud adrift on its untroubled blue.

Then he saw the fence where it joined the gulch to make a trap for the two wild horses. He listened for some sound from above. But all was quiet, and Gil surmised that when the cornered outlaws struck the fence they had turned away toward Devil's Gulch, on the other side—or they might even be racing back, in sheer defiance, toward that line of riders.

Gil left his saddle and found a seat on a nearby rock. Perhaps, if the outlaws did break back and Fealy missed them, it would give the tail-end men a chance. If that happened, Dad would blame him for not being there. Someone would rope the horses sure enough, and maybe he had been a chump, sneaking off like this. A chickenhearted guy like him probably never would get to school.

Then, so suddenly it made him jump, he heard a close-up repetition of the great black stallion's unforgettable, trumpeting challenge.

Leaping hastily to his feet, Gil gazed upward, and there above him on the rim saw the wide, red nostrils and gleaming eyes of the cornered Prince. Beside that proud black head appeared the froth-flecked nose of the little sorrel, quivering nostrils widespread in terror, and panic-stricken, liquid gaze fixed intently on her mate.

For one brief, disdainful instant, Black Prince glanced back across his shoulder, then touched the sorrel's nose with his, in command and encouragement so clear that it seemed to Gil the Prince had spoken. In the next split second, the stallion leaped—a jump that no man in his wildest fancy would dream a horse could make.

Not a dozen feet from where the boy stood, the outlaw stallion struck the arroyo bottom, a blur of black, slashed by four whitely gleaming hoofs. Gil shut his eyes, believing that when he looked he would see the Black Prince lying dead.

Then he heard the stallion call again and, opening his eyes, saw the Prince unhurt, and realized that the streak of red flashing downward between himself and the strip of sky was the mare, who had followed her lord and master.

But now, as the red streak came to earth, both the slender forelegs buckled, and with a little moaning cry, the mare went over on her side.

Black Prince, already turned for flight, was caught back instantly by the sound, and Gil stood frozen as he saw the stallion dip his nose and hold it long against his mate's. There was no hope for the mare, Gil thought, and believed Black Prince knew it, too.

Gil could have run to fetch his rope from where his prick-eared pony stood, not a dozen feet away. He could have flung his loop easily about Black Prince's drooping neck, and the stricken stallion would not have stirred. The thought

flashed into Gil's mind, but he didn't ponder it long. All his attention was centered on the dreadful plight of the sorrel mare.

A sound, intruding from above, broke the spell—for Gil, at least. Looking up, he saw Jim Fealy on his thoroughbred, and other men behind him—Protheroe, and the elder Fealy, and the short fat man Gil didn't know.

A sudden rage welled up in Gil as he saw Jim Fealy grab his rope. The Prince had heard—he must have heard, with those ears attuned to the slightest sound—but he stood his ground by the fallen mare, an easy and certain target for the loop that Jim was hastily building.

In a blur, Gil saw Jim swing and throw, saw the rope uncoil and angle downward. In another instant, that hissing and distended loop would close about Black Prince's neck—that drooping black neck, no longer proud and arched with triumph.

In that instant, Gil came to life. Leaping wildly from the clump of brush which had sheltered his observation point, he swung his father's old black hat, jumping wildly up and down and screaming as if his lungs would burst, "Run! Run, Black Prince! You've got to run!"

Startled, the stallion turned his head, and Jim Fealy's hissing loop slid harmlessly down a sleek black shoulder.

Gil could hear Jim's shouted curse. Protheroe was swearing, too. But Gil didn't care. For mingled with their shouts was another sound—the sudden flurry of scrambling hoofs, as the red mare, panicked by all the noise, rose to her unsteady legs—legs not broken, after all—legs she could move on slowly now—then more swiftly, as the Black Prince, circling, nipped her gently on the flank. And then, in a wonderful rising thunder of drumming hoofs, the two of them were making off down the sandy floor of Big Arroyo.

It was some time before the men above could circle down to the spot where Gil was numbly waiting. He wasn't sure what they would do. They might even put him in jail for this. Yet he had never felt so glad, and sort of right and good inside. And when they all came pounding up, Gil stood his ground.

"The Prince was really mine," he said, in answer to Jim Fealy's accusation. "I could have put my loop around his neck long before you showed up. But I wanted him to get away, and I'm glad he did."

Both Protheroe and the Fealys were black with anger and making threats. At last, however, they drifted off. Then the short, fat man came up to Gil with outstretched hand.

"I'm fond of horses, too," he said. "I'd like to know you better, son. I've made excuses to Fealy, and I'd like to ride along to your place for dinner if you'll invite me."

Gil said, "All right. I know the folks will be glad to have you." But the folks, Gil thought, would be disappointed in their son, and sorry about the prize—not understanding how a boy could want a thing as much as he had wanted to go off to school, then have his chance, and let it go.

The fat man's name was Myers. But it wasn't till late in the afternoon that Gil learned he was the cattle buyer whom Dad had failed to land.

At the dinner table, all the talk had been about the hunt and the two wild horses. Finally Gil had left to do his chores. Myers was gone when he came back, and his father was waiting impatiently to tell him that though Myers had signed for the Fealy cattle, he had bought theirs, too, this afternoon—every last one that was fit for market.

When Dad handed the check to Gil, his voice was husky. "It's yours—for school," he said. And

Ma's eyes were brimming with joyful tears.

That made it pretty hard for Gil. After all, when a fellow is almost a grown man, and going away to school, he can't be blubbering in front of his folks.

Eleanor Hoffmann

Fiesta Parade

"Ten minutes late already," muttered Julie Clark, staring impatiently at the empty track.

Her father, taking his hand off the wheel of the station wagon, laid it on hers. With a contrite smile she apologized.

"I'm sorry, Dad. Don't think I'm not looking forward to Kate's visit. Of course I am! I think it's wonderful that we can have her here for fiesta. Poor little kid! It must be awful to have one leg in a brace and have to use a cane."

Mrs. Clark nodded. "Kate's going to need all the extra love her family and friends can give her until she gets back to normal."

"I know," said Julie, "only . . ."

"Only time's getting short before the great day," her father said with his so nearly perfect understanding, "and you still have a lot to do at the ranch to make Topaz's silver saddle glitter as brightly as his golden skin."

That was exactly it—at least part of it. Julie needed every minute of these last three days for grooming her beautiful Topaz and rubbing up the silver *conchas* on his saddle so that in the whole long fiesta parade of five hundred horses, no animal would glitter like her dazzling young palomino. And here she was wasting time in the city, twenty miles from her beloved Santa Inez Valley ranch.

Her father and mother knew this. What they did not know was what her neighbor Bob Howland had said to her in his casual way yesterday in the village post office.

"Hi, Julie, how about getting together on slicking up our horses and gear for the fiesta?" Of course he might not have meant a word of it. He had a way of holding out heaven like that and never consummating the gift. He had done it last summer before he went off to college, and now this summer he was doing it again. How many times had she seen a puzzled look in his blue eyes? As if he wanted to do the things he suggested, then, when the time came, something that was not indifference held him back.

Was there something wrong with her that she could never bring these dates off? Could her mother be right in saying sixteen was too old to be a tomboy? Occasionally she gave this possibility secret and serious thought. So she was a tomboy! Preferred horses to people; the corral to the house; blue jeans to ballerina skirts; horse talk to high school chitchat! So what? That was the way she was made. If she wasn't that way, she wasn't herself. She was somebody else. She was a phony. She was herself when she was riding fence with her father, training Topaz, roping calves at stock shows.

Now suppose Bob actually did turn up to polish saddles with her as he had suggested. It would be the first date she had ever had with him! And even if it wasn't a date such as going dancing, it was something that might lead to their riding side by side in the parade—he on his ivory palomino mare Chiquita, she on her golden beauty Topaz. But with nine-year-old Kate making a third, it couldn't be the same as having him to herself.

Don't be a selfish pig, she admonished herself, and at that moment a whistle hooted down the track.

When the train stopped, Julie was the first to spot a small, pale child being helped down between porter and conductor. At Julie's shout, her father came running to take Kate tenderly in his strong arms. By the time Mr. Clark had stood the child gently on the ground, Mrs. Clark had her arms around her.

"Welcome, Kate darling. We're so happy to have you."

Julie offered a sunburned paw. To her confusion, Kate, leaning against her for support, raised her thin arms and lifted her face to be kissed. In the station wagon, unaware of Julie's embarrassment, her little cousin settled back affectionately against her shoulder. As the most efficient of her father's ranch hands, Julie was as averse to emotional display as any cowboy in the bunkhouse.

"Here's where the fiesta parade starts." Julie pointed out a gigantic grandstand rising on the water front. "Dad has seats for you and Mother in one of the best boxes."

"For me?" repeated Kate. "Won't you be there too?"

"Me? Goodness no! You can look for me riding with the Santa Inez palominos. I broke and trained my new colt Topaz just in time. Dad will be riding his champion quarter horse Red Tony."

Kate was all interest. "Before I was sick," she said eagerly, "I had a pony and rode in a parade at home. It was the most wonderful thing I've ever done."

While Julie fumbled uncomfortably for an answer, her father pointed out the mountain ridge that lay between the city and the valley ranch.

By the time they had crossed San Marcos Pass and had wound down through the oak-bordered roads to the ranch house, supper was on the table. Afterward Kate looked even whiter and more frail than when Mr. Clark had lifted her off the train, and Mrs. Clark recommended bed.

"But I want to see Topaz first," begged Kate.

"I'll ride up to your window if you like," Julie suggested.

Kate turned dark, pleading eyes toward her. "Do, please, do!"

Like a golden tongue of flame in the last glow of the sunset, Topaz came galloping across the corral. His happy whinny answered Julie's call. His soft nostrils sought the hollow of her throat as she lifted the bridle over his head. For a minute she laid her cheek close against his, then hoisted herself up to his saddleless back and galloped up to the house, reining in smartly just outside Kate's room.

"Oh, Julie," sighed Kate, rapturously reaching out through the window to touch the golden head. "How beautiful he is!"

Julie, changing Topaz from gait to gait, from right to left lead, backing and swinging into figure eights, was not as collected and cool as she looked. A feeling of embarrassment, even of guilt, at her own strength and happiness kept her silent. It was a relief when her mother called Kate to bed and she was free.

Later that evening Mrs. Clark said, "Kate has a fearful crush on you, Julie. If you were a movie queen, she couldn't be your more ardent fan. If she's sentimental and demonstrative, don't hurt her by being gruff."

"Of course not," Julie answered.

But as she reached her own room, she wasn't

so sure that she could handle a crush gracefully. "I'm no movie queen!" she said to herself, as she kicked off her blue jeans. "What do I want with fans?"

At breakfast the next morning, Kate asked. "Are you going to ride Topaz all morning, Julie?"

"Not until I get some more of the silver on his saddle polished for the parade."

"Silver!" Kate's eyes brightened. "I love to polish silver! I always help Mother. Let me help you."

"Thanks, but . . . I don't think you'll be very comfortable down by the corral. You'd . . ." At the look of disappointment on Kate's face Julie checked herself. "I could bring my saddle and bridle up to the front porch and we could put them on a table."

"Tell me more about the parade," demanded Kate later, as she rubbed away at the *conchas* on Topaz's bridle. "Are there really five hundred horses? Is there music? Are there floats?"

Julie was in the midst of describing the floats when a clatter of hoofs made both girls look up.

"Hello there," called Bob Howland, pulling

his ivory palomino mare to a neat stop and dismounting.

"Hi," answered Julie, color creeping up her cheeks. She presented him to Kate, and he delighted the little girl by bending over her hand as if she were a grown lady.

"Mother sent me over with a bag of nectarines," he said. "How's the polishing going?" His finger touched the glittering silver cap of the saddle horn.

"Okay," mumbled Julie, stealing a look at the saddle on Chiquita's ivory back for comparison. But Chiquita was wearing a workday roping saddle.

"Julie," Mrs. Clark called from the house, "there's a pitcher of lemonade in the refrigerator."

"Thanks a lot," said Bob, "but I've got to get back pronto and help Dad. We're still having trouble finding drivers for a couple of our old carriages. Everybody who can handle a horse would rather ride. So long, Julie. Good-by, Kate. You're a grand little polisher."

At the compliment, a faint flush of pink crept into Kate's pale cheeks. With shining eyes she watched Bob swing himself into the saddle and disappear through the oaks.

"Isn't he just about the best-looking boy you've ever seen?" she asked dreamily.

"Oh, I don't know," Julie answered with a shrug, her head bent low, her cheeks burning with embarrassment.

"Is he going to ride in the parade?"

"Bob? Of course. He's practically running it. His father's chairman of the fiesta committee and the family is lending their collection of old coaches and carriages."

Now, because Kate's head was bent again over the polishing, Julie dared turn her eyes wistfully in the direction of the fading hoofbeats. Would he have stayed to help shine up her saddle, if he had found her alone down at the corral?

"Will Bob lead the parade?"

Julie shook her head.

"Where will he ride?"

"With the Santa Inez Valley palominos."

"Beside you?"

"How do I know?" In her effort to make her voice natural, she sounded gruff. If only Kate would change the subject!

"Did you ride in the parade last year?" the little girl asked.

"Last year and the year before and every year they've had it. I've never missed one."

"Lucky Julie! Go on, tell me some more about it."

While Julie's thoughts followed Bob Howland through the oaks and sycamores, she heard herself talking parade and more parade till the sun stood overhead.

"Are we going to polish the silver on your saddle this morning?" asked Kate hopefully the next day at breakfast.

Julie shook her head emphatically. "Topaz lost a shoe last night. I have to ride him over to Solvang and get him shod." At the look of disappointment on Kate's face, she turned away quickly.

"Can't take him till about noon, Miss Julie," said Helmer Hansen, the blacksmith in the little Danish town of Solvang.

"Okay with me!" Julie grinned. Around the corner stood Mrs. Johannsen's bakery, famous as far south as Hollywood for its Danish pastries.

After a delectable lunch of almond *Schaum*

Torte and pastry whirls that broke every rule of balanced diet, Julie collected a second assortment of the fanciest *Danska* confections to take back to Kate.

On the ride back, the white face of her little cousin kept superimposing itself upon every gay fiesta image. Julie tried to imagine herself watching the parade instead of taking part in it. Horrible thought!

As she cantered up past the corral of the house, she wished she had something more to offer Kate than just something to eat. If it could only be a gift of some of her own buoyant strength and vitality!

The station wagon was gone from the shady spot under the oak tree. Suddenly Julie remembered with horror that her parents were due in Santa Barbara for a fiesta committee luncheon. By staying in Solvang, she had left Kate alone for lunch.

"Hi, Kate!" she called swinging down from the saddle.

No answer. "Tying" Topaz to the ground, she took the porch steps two at a time. Living room and library were both empty. In the kitchen old Adelfa was shaping cornhusks for tamales.

"Did Miss Kate go into Santa Barbara with Mother and Dad?" asked Julie.

Adelfa shook her head. "*La pobrecita*, the poor little one. Santa Maria, it is sad to be so lame. She is in her room—crying."

"Crying," repeated Julie aghast. "She must be homesick! Couldn't you—"

"She has locked her door," interrupted Adelfa.

Without waiting to hear any more, Julie rushed through the hallway. Outside Kate's door she stopped to listen. Old Adelfa was right. There was a distinct though muffled sound of sobbing. Julie wrinkled her forehead. How could she fix it so Kate wouldn't know she had heard the crying?

"Hi, Kate," she called gaily. "As soon as I get Topaz unsaddled, I've got a surprise for you. Meet me on the porch."

Five minutes later, she found Kate waiting on the porch. Pretending not to notice the freshly washed face and the red eyes, she presented her with the Solvang pastries. With fingers that showed no eager curiosity, Kate undid the string and opened the box.

"Thank you, Julie; thank you very much," Kate said gravely.

"Well," said Julie, awkward and embarrassed at the failure of her present, "watch out you don't eat so many that you have to miss the fiesta."

At the word "fiesta," Kate's chin suddenly began to tremble. Though Julie looked quickly away, she caught sight of a tear rolling down each cheek. Her arm went around Kate. That was easy. To find words was something else.

"Go on, Kate. Have a good cry. I'd be homesick myself if I were in your place."

"I'm not homesick," moaned Kate. Julie's arm was too much for her self-control.

"Well, what then? Tell me." With a hand that until now had patted only horses and dogs, Julie stroked the hot, tear-sticky cheek. "What is it, Katie?"

"It's . . . it's . . . the fiesta," sobbed Kate, "the lovely, wonderful fiesta."

"But, darling, you're going to see it. Dad's got the two best seats in the whole grandstand for you and Mother."

"I . . . I . . . don't want to *see* it," Kate wailed. "I want to be in it, like you!"

Of course, that was it, Julie told herself. I ought to have known. That's the way I would have felt. But what could be done?

A car horn sounded. The station wagon was coming up through the oaks.

Kate pulled herself free of Julie's arm. "Don't tell them," she begged. "Don't tell them I cried about wanting to be in the fiesta. Promise. You've *got* to promise."

"All right, Kate, I promise, but . . ."

Kate hadn't waited to hear the end. By the time the car had stopped, she was gone.

What a dumb promise, was all Julie could think of as she listened absent-mindedly to her parents' account of the luncheon. Suddenly something her mother was saying caught Julie's attention.

"The Howlands are still having trouble finding someone to drive their favorite carriage. Nobody wants to drive. Why, where's Kate?" she interrupted herself. "Did Adelfa give you both a good lunch?"

"I . . ." Julie hesitated, "I think Kate's having a nap. Look, Mum, I have to go down and water Topaz. I'll be right back."

More important than watering Topaz was the need to be alone and think. An idea had pounced unasked into her mind, and, in spite of herself, was taking a firmer and firmer hold. She, Julie

Clark, could handle a horse between the shafts of a carriage as well as under the saddle, and she had broken Topaz for both saddle and carriage.

In the tackroom the sparkling silver *conchas* of the saddle caught her eye. She saw herself and Topaz prancing up State Street beside an ivory palomino mare named Chiquita. Then she saw another picture—an old-fashioned carriage decorated from wheels to shafts with flowers; beside the driver sat a child so happy that her usually white cheeks were the color of pink roses. Like colored slides shown over and over again, these two images alternated before her mind's eye.

Fifteen minutes later, she rejoined her parents on the porch.

"Well, sister, what's on your mind?" asked her father.

"I . . . Well, I was wondering if Kate wouldn't like to be *in* the parade instead of just watching it. And so I thought perhaps—well, you know I've been in a lot of parades and I'll be in a lot more, so I thought maybe if I harnessed Topaz to the Howlands' carriage and drove him, then Kate could ride beside me. Do you think that would be okay with the Howlands?"

"Okay with them? They'll be delighted!" exclaimed her father. "Why, Julie, Kate will be wild with joy!"

"It's a lovely, generous thought, Julie," said her mother.

What a hypocrite their praise made her feel. If she could only tell them that without Kate's tears, she never would have thought of it. But a promise was a promise.

"Will you call the Howlands?" she muttered, embarrassed.

"With pleasure," said her father.

"Now we'll have to think of a costume for you," said her mother.

"Costume!" repeated Julie in a tone of deep disgust. It was bad enough to have to ride in a carriage without being tricked out in Spanish lace and stuff.

'I guess you're in for it, pet," said her father. "Strict committee rules. Spanish costumes in all the floats and carriages."

"Okay," she grunted miserably. "Only thing I can think of worse than having to wear it, is having to make it."

"Don't worry, darling," said her mother, delighted at the chance of getting her daughter out of blue jeans. "You needn't touch needle or thread."

"Spanish flounces! Ugh!" muttered Julie, as she headed for Kate's room with a better offering than Danish pastry.

"Oh, Julie, Julie!" Kate exclaimed at the news. "Beside you in the fiesta! How absolutely lovely! But didn't you want to ride Topaz?"

Julie made her speech about all the fiestas she had been in and all the ones to come so convincingly that Kate's eyes sparkled with happiness. And I put that shining look into them, thought Julie, suddenly feeling strange and surprised and happy herself.

For Julie this new happiness kept coming and going like clouds across the sun. It disappeared the next day when her father's Red Tony with his saddle and her own Topaz without a saddle were loaded into the two-horse trailer to go ahead into Santa Barbara.

And the next morning, the great day itself, as her mother completed her Spanish costume, Julie scowled into the mirror.

"All dressed up like a monkey," she grumbled to herself.

But when Kate exclaimed, "Oh, Julie, I never

saw anyone so beautiful!" Julie let the little girl think the compliment had pleased her. Wasn't this Kate's day? Let every minute of it be bright and shining for her.

In Santa Barbara the out-of-town crowds were already thick on streets and sidewalks. At the entrance to the improvised stable and corral which the Howlands shared with the Clarks, they could see Mrs. Howland supervising the loading of an old stagecoach with forty-niners.

"Here's your carriage, Julie," Mrs. Howland called, beckoning the Clarks through the crowd of gawking visitors. "How pretty you look. Let one of the boys harness Topaz for you. You mustn't spoil that lovely dress!"

"I won't hurt it."

"No, Julie," said her mother. "Mrs. Howland is right."

That's the trouble with these monkey clothes, thought Julie, as she rebelliously watched one of the Howland ranch hands back Topaz between the shafts of a carriage gaily decked with red roses.

"Oh, Julie, what fun! What lovely fun!" sang Kate, as they headed for the waterfront at Topaz's smartest trot.

But in front of them and behind them cantered the proud riders, and Julie smarted under their pride. Not until she and Kate moved into their waiting place at the water front did they begin to see other wheeled vehicles—the floats, the carriages, the mule teams, and the oxcarts.

Suddenly above the clatter of hoofs and the sound of the police cars rose the drums and the trumpets of the band. Section after section moved up into place and the head of the great parade began to wind its way past the applause of the grandstand. Now the bearded prospectors with picks, shovels, and burros fell into place; now the Santa Inez palominos with sunlight dancing on polished hides and silver saddles; now the flower-decorated carriages.

With the tip of Julie's whip tickling his golden neck, Topaz pranced ahead into the procession.

In the long block before they reached the grandstand, Julie had all she could do to soothe the excited colt. When someone shouted "Bravo!" and threw a rose that hit his haunches, his front feet left the ground. As he reared up high on his hind legs, his shrill squeal cut across the applause.

"Quiet, boy! Steady, Topaz!" Julie commanded, sitting straight and collected, though her heart pounded.

She was too intent on keeping Topaz in hand to care whether the applause of the grandstand was for the palominos in front of her, for the section of flower-decorated carriages that she was leading, or for her own skillful driving. Now she had him under control, still quivering, but at least with all four feet on the ground. As she released her tense hold on the reins, the shadow of a rider fell across the dashboard.

"Good going, Julie!" Bob Howland, transformed into a young Spanish don, complete with guitar, came prancing up beside her.

So he isn't riding with the Santa Inez palominos after all, she thought. What is he doing—cantering up and down like a sheepdog seeing that we all keep in line?

Because Topaz was behaving beautifully now—as if he enjoyed parading two Spanish beauties in a carriage covered with red roses—she dared shift her glance, first to see if Kate had been frightened, then to meet Bob's smile. Maybe it was her silly costume, maybe it was because she had to play up to Kate's admiration, but somehow she found herself returning Bob's smile as

easily as if looking at him had never choked up everything natural inside her.

"Ah, Senorita," Bob began, stepping into the character of his Spanish costume with a flourish of his tasseled hat, "the red roses with which I decorated your carriage blush with envy at your loveliness."

"Thank you, sir," she heard herself saying smoothly. Now, she thought, now he will prance up to join the palominos ahead and pay their riders lovely Spanish compliments.

But to her surprise he seemed to be checking the mare's eagerness to dance forward. He moved up closer to the carriage and their eyes met. All trace of his puzzled uncertainty had vanished. "I've been waiting for a certain tomboy to grow up," he said for her ears alone. "You're beautiful, Julie."

Ahead the Santa Inez palominos slowed down. Burnished saddles sparkled; hides glinted like new gold; horse-proud riders posed for a hundred cameras.

Vivian Breck

A Touch of Arab

Usually the day we rode into the canyon to open the ranger cabin was the happiest of the whole year. On that day my father stopped being Professor Mallory of the Geology Department and changed into Ranger Mallory of Merced Canyon—and I had Cirque to ride. After a little time in the Sierra Nevada you get used to the light, but on the day you ride in the sun seems so near, and shines so gold-and-silver bright, that it stirs you up inside. The mountains have a sparkle on them.

Always before—and that's eleven summers, because we have been going to the Merced cabin ever since my mother died when I was three—

Ranger Mallory's eyes would get sort of big behind his glasses and the tip of his nose would quiver at the smell of wild azaleas in Little Yosemite. He'd crack silly jokes as we rode and call himself "Old Sourdough." But this year he looked as if he had just flunked one of his favorite students.

"Look at Cirque, Daddy," I said. "Isn't he beautiful? He's so glad to be out of pasture he wants to dance uphill." Cirque is a Western stock horse with just a touch of Arab. That makes him strong and dependable and brave, but a little flashy, too—he likes to prance.

But Daddy didn't seem to appreciate Cirque's polished granite coat and lovely legs. Surely, I thought, after we climb the zigzags and get to foaming water, or to where we can see the Clark Range, we will get his mountain face. The Clark Range looks like black starched fringe combed straight up against the sky. We think it's very exciting.

It was when we stopped for lunch that Daddy told me. We had built a cooking fire and were waiting for the water to boil for tea when he said, "I wish you'd stop trying to balance yourself on that branch, Meggie. I really don't want an acrobat for a daughter. Besides, I need to talk to you." He kept digging at the damp crust of pine needles on the ground as he spoke. "I'm sorry, Meg, but this is going to be a mighty short summer."

"What on earth do you mean?" I asked him. "It's not even July yet."

"But this year I'm having just a two-week businessman's vacation." He put his hand on my arm. "Meg, my dear," he said almost pleadingly, "I do hope you'll understand." Then he told me that he had resigned from the Forest Service to accept a job teaching at summer session, and that he wanted me to go to a girls' camp.

"I don't want you growing up one-sided," he said, "with no interests outside of your riding. You must cultivate other enthusiasms. You need friendship with boys and girls your own age. That's why I want you to go to this camp and make an honest effort to get along with the other girls and join in all their different activities."

"But Cirque!" I cried. "Darling Cirque! What will we do—"

"A professor's salary is not designed to include boarding a horse in town," Daddy answered slowly. "I'm sorry, but I think the time has come when we'll have to sell Cirque. Surely you wouldn't want to keep an educated young gentleman at pasture indefinitely. Would you, Meggie?"

I shook my head, but deep inside I knew there was more behind this selling Cirque than just money. Several times that spring I had cut school to practice for the gymkhana, and when Daddy found out about it he'd looked pretty grim.

"Education," he had said to me, his jaw particularly square, "is the bones of life. Without it you may grow up bright and pretty, but sometime life will crumble on you because you haven't the right bones underneath."

"Why do you have to be a professor all over your private life?" I'd railed. "You know I'm going to live on a ranch and raise stock horses. What's analyzing *The Merchant of Venice* got to do with that?"

"Quite a lot," Daddy had said, and I knew there was no use arguing with him.

After that miserable lunch on the trail we rode the rest of the fourteen miles to our cabin trying to talk about things that wouldn't hurt too much. But as we passed the granite slide where the Merced tumbles down in foaming sheets of water, I couldn't help remembering old Mr. Scripps.

"Did they ever find him?" I had to ask.

"Yes, they did," Daddy answered, as if rushing water were no longer beautiful. "At the bottom of Nevada Falls. There will be one advantage to our short summer, anyhow."

"How could there be?"

"I probably won't have to hunt for any lost fishermen or campers."

Usually when we arrive at the Ranger Station I want to squeal for joy. Our brown log cabin looks so welcoming, under the Jeffrey pines! This year I could only wonder whose name would be tacked up on the bulletin board where the little metal sign, "Ranger Arthur B. Mallory," had hung for so long. Cirque was all for dashing upstream to see if the big bridge, where the Lyell Fork joins the Merced, had lasted out the winter. Since the trail gang put a concrete pier under the bridge it has never washed out, but before that every time we had a heavy storm the melted snow, swirling down in torrents from the upper falls, had carried the bridge with it. I unsaddled Cirque and turned him into the corral beside the cabin, then went inside to unpack. What I really wanted to do was bury my face in a pillow, or run across the river on my log and crawl into the underbrush, where the does hide their new fawns.

It was silly for Daddy to think that getting rid of Cirque would make me spend more time with what he calls "comrades of my own age." Those dopes! Last year he practically drove me to join a sort of dancing club. The dancing part wasn't bad—dancing is pretty good exercise. But the girls were so silly and the boys so juvenile in their conversation, I only went once. But it had never occurred to me that my not going to dances, and being bored by my schoolmates, would get mixed up in Daddy's mind with my loving Cirque so much. How could I make him understand the way I felt about my darling? My father wouldn't sell *me*, no matter how much I cost to keep!

Suddenly an idea hit me. Cirque looks especially beautiful standing on his hind legs or jumping. If, every day for two weeks, Daddy had to watch my horse doing extra-special, prancy tricks, perhaps—

I raced into the cabin for my lucky tee shirt—the blue-and-white striped one I wore when I won the bareback hackamore race at the gymkhana. Then I jerked the top bars off the corral gate, and made Cirque jump so that every muscle showed under his glossy coat. Finally, to rest him, we practiced a kind of circus trick I have been wanting to learn. That was when Wake came along.

Right next to our cabin is a mammoth Jeffrey pine with one branch overhanging the corral. I stood on Cirque's back (that isn't hard if you have grippy toes and are used to climbing over logs) and swung myself to the overhanging branch. The hard part was dropping down again on Cirque's back while he was loping by. I was riding around standing up when I spotted something that looked like a great blue heron—all legs, with a hump on top—leaning against the corral, one of his legs wound around the other. When I rode over, the hump turned out to be a knapsack, and the heron asked, "Can I take a picture of you doing that stunt? You're a wonderful color. Like the ocean—extremely clean blue-and-white."

"I don't mind," I said, wondering whether he meant that my shirt looked like the ocean, or my face. My eyes are violently blue, and my eyebrows and hair looked mighty pale against my sun-browned skin.

While he set up a tripod Cirque and I did our trick over and over.

"What's your horse's name?" he asked.

"Cirque."

"Circ, for circus?"

"Circus nothing! He's a mountain horse. His name is C-i-r-q-u-e. Don't you know any geology? A cirque is the round place hollowed out of the granite at the head of a stream by a glacier. You ought to study geology," I told him. "It makes the mountains much more interesting."

He said he doubted if he'd ever have time.

That was Wake. His whole name was Wakefield Bender. He was seventeen, and this was his first trip into the Sierra Nevada. He had heard that the Merced, just below the Ranger cabin, was full of cascades running between granite cliffs, and he thought they would make interesting pictures.

Daddy suggested I help him choose a place to camp. It was lucky I did. Wake didn't know any more about the woods than I know about photography.

"This looks like a fine place to hang my hat," he announced at the place where the trail crossed Rafferty Creek, two minutes from our cabin. "I'd like to wake up in the morning looking at those big black rocks sticking out through the bubbles."

"You'll wake up in a puddle, if it rains," I told him. "Rafferty catches a tremendous runoff. It spreads out all over the place after a shower."

As he was looking back at the foam of water he stumbled and nearly went flat. If I had known how easy it was for Wake to stumble I never would have cut through the woods on a deer trail! He laughed about his clumsiness, though, even when a rock sent him sprawling. I couldn't help laughing, too. He looked so silly with his heron legs waving in the air.

"Your legs remind me of Alice and her neck," I said. "They've grown so fast you don't know how to manage them."

"Quick!" he shouted. "Find me a mushroom to nibble!"

After that we were easy together. Somehow, when people too old for fairy tales both like *Alice in Wonderland* it gives them the feeling of being old friends.

The place I had in mind for Wake's camp didn't suit him at all. "This has no character," he objected.

"But look at the firewood! And it has perfect screening from the wind."

He still shook his head. "It's just shrubbery.

I want to camp where the outlook has form—composition of some kind. A picture to live with."

Finally he made camp on a granite shelf, where little crooked pines grow out of the cracks in the rock. As I watched him unpack I hoped he had food in his knapsack as well as camera stuff, because he was awfully thin. You could see his shoulder blades right through his shirt. I couldn't help liking him. He had nice brown eyes that looked straight at you—that is, when one of them wasn't covered up with a piece of rumply hair. I asked him why he hadn't gotten a haircut before he came away.

"There wasn't time," he said. "And anyhow, I'd spent all my allowance on film."

Wake walked over to our cabin quite often to watch me jumping Cirque, and sometimes I rode past his camp to tell him about something I thought he might like to photograph. I never picked the things he wanted, though. It was the cascades that fascinated him. They were difficult to photograph because the canyon walls are so steep, and he was anxious to explore the other side of the river for a better angle, so one day I showed him where my log crosses. My log—I call it mine because I've used it so many years—is the only way over the Merced between our cabin and the big junction bridge five miles upstream. Wake said he wished he could skitter about fallen trees the way I do. His legs reminded me of a colt's—they wouldn't quite obey him.

We had several conversations before I asked him about dancing. I wanted to know if he thought dancing was important for a girl to learn, the way Daddy seemed to think it was.

"I certainly don't think it's important," he told me. "Most girls at dances are so silly I can't find anything to talk to them about. I only go to parties myself because I don't wish to become a recluse."

If Wake felt tongue-tied at dances I decided I needn't bother with them, either. Because certainly Wake had more ideas to the minute than anyone I'd ever known, except my father.

Half our businessman's vacation was gone when the first storm broke. It had been building for two days, but I couldn't make Wake believe that those cloudy afternoons meant that the sky would pour down buckets of water some day soon. First the clouds grew gray, then black. Daddy looked at the barometer and put the fattest chunk of pine he could find into our stove. Big drops began to spatter against the glass, hitting slowly at first, in little spurts between the gusts of wind. Then the wind came roaring down off the Clark Range and whole sheets of water pounded the windows.

We could almost see the river rising as every crack and gully on the canyon walls filled with rain and melted snow. I knew my log would soon be under water—might even be swept away. After a little while the rain changed to hail—big, mountain hail, like moth balls. I thought the windowpanes would shatter.

But if the rain comes fast, it never lasts long. The minute the storm was over I went out to see how Cirque was. He looked pretty shivery, huddled against Daddy's horse in one corner of the corral. Even his beautiful tail was droopy.

"How about a good run to warm up?" I asked him.

His ears said, "Let's go!"

I was wondering about Wake, too, remembering the casual way he'd anchored his pup tent to a couple of twiggy bushes. If his bedding was wet I thought it would be friendly to invite him into the cabin to dry off. I was sure Daddy wouldn't mind, though he always says we can't take in all the campers in the Sierra to dry off every time it rains.

I jumped on Cirque bareback and we galloped down the trail to where I could see Wake's tent. The granite sand was still full of puddles that splashed as we tore along, and Cirque skidded to a quick stop with his forefeet in the air. He's glorious when he does that. I wished Daddy could have seen him.

"Hi, Wake!" I shouted. "Did you get all your stuff under cover?" When nobody answered I crashed Cirque right across the dead timber to Wake's camp. He wasn't there. All his things were spread around outside the tent, soaking wet, so I knew he must have been off taking pictures when it began to rain.

Suddenly I was frightened. I don't think I ever felt really frightened in the mountains before. Daddy never let us get into jams, because he knows ahead of time where danger lies; but Wake was such a baby in the woods, slipping and stumbling, never paying any attention to where he was going because he was so busy thinking about his lovely pictures. I was sure he had gone to photograph the cascades, for he'd been talking about them so much, never satisfied with the shots he had already made.

My heels dug into Cirque, and he bounded straight ahead, like a deer through underbrush. I headed for my log because I was positive that was where Wake had crossed the river. The Merced had risen at least ten inches, and the current was so strong that even a champion swimmer would have been dashed over the falls. It was sweeping across the top of the log now, and I dared not try to cross on it.

Then I saw his head—the rest of him was under water. I'm never going to forget the way his eyes looked. They were wide open and glinty, like a wild animal's facing a light at night. With one hand he was clinging to a branch of driftwood that had wedged against my log; with the other, he was trying to hold his camera out of the water. He saw me, too, but I knew he couldn't hear my voice. The water was so loud it drowned the sound.

There was no time to go for Daddy. Wake was on the upstream side of the log, but the driftwood he was clinging to might come loose any minute. Then the water would sweep him right under the log. If that happened he wouldn't have a chance.

Not against the cascades. I thought of old Mr. Scripps washing the whole way down to Nevada Falls. Cirque and I were going to have to get Wake out! There wasn't any other way. "Please, God," I prayed, "make the driftwood stick together until we get there."

Cirque understood too, I think. He began quivering all over as I urged him right to the edge of the river. "Come on, Cirque," I whispered, wishing my bare heels were spurs. In a moment the current was swirling around his knees. He planted his forefeet on the bottom and refused to budge.

"Cirque!" I cried. "We've got to get Wake out of there quickly!"

He lowered his head, sniffling the roily brown water, then looked around at me as if he were saying, "Meg, old girl, it's too much for us. The old Merced is too strong for you and me."

A terrible gust of wind whipped the branches of a tree against my face. I realized then exactly what I would have to do. Without my weight Cirque stood a chance of crossing the river. But he would have to be driven forcibly into the water. I leaned as far forward as I could and screamed at Wake, "Catch Cirque's tail!" Then

I stood up on Cirque's back and grabbed the tree branch with one hand. With one foot I whacked him across the rump with all my might and bellowed, "Go on, Cirque!" Startled, he lunged into the stream, while I swung over the water. It was hard getting my legs up on the branch, because it wasn't steady like the pine over the corral. But finally I made it.

Blessed Cirque. He understood. He waded out as far as he could toward Wake, and all I could do was to sit there, biting blood out of my lips. When the current took him he began to swim, struggling with all his brave stock-horse heart against the flood water. Wake had to let his camera go, but he caught Cirque's tail and the horse dragged him, slowly but surely, up on the other side.

I thought, of course, that Wake would jump on Cirque and ride to the junction bridge and back to the Ranger cabin for Daddy. But I could see that he was too exhausted to move.

Cirque stood over him, sniffing with his velvet nose. Then he pawed the ground as if he were saying, "Come on! My mistress can't hang on that branch forever." But Wake just lay there, shivering. Cirque tossed his head and whinnied

—then crashed off into the underbrush alone. It's five miles to the junction bridge and five miles back on our side of the river, so I knew I'd have to hang on a good long time. But I never supposed any time would *feel* so long. I tried to settle myself more comfortably in the crotch of the tree, and watched the mad waters swirling around the trunk.

Daddy came at last. He lassoed me with a rope, then threw another rope over the branch for me to shinny down. When I felt the ground under my feet again and Daddy's arms around me, I got silly and cried. He tossed me up in back of his saddle, and all the way back to the cabin I hugged him around the waist, tight, the way I used to ride when I was a little girl. Daddy said Cirque must have galloped every inch of the way. He'd come to the corral fence lathered with sweat, in spite of the icy wind, and Daddy had known right away, when he saw him riderless, that something had happened to me.

"Get yourself warm, Meg; then put plenty of water on to heat and fill every bottle you can lay your hands on. Make a hot drink," he called back as he dashed out the door, "and warm some blankets in front of the fire."

I was so busy carrying out his instructions that it didn't seem any time before he was back with the still dripping Wake. Daddy took off Wake's clothes, bundled him into a pair of flannel pajamas, and wrapped him in the warm blankets lined with bottles of hot water. In a little while he was able to sit up and take the hot drink, and by evening he was enjoying the huge meal we brought to him on a tray.

The next morning I was getting breakfast in the kitchen when Daddy came in with a load of wood. "I can't wait any longer to ask you, Dad," I said, putting down the coffee I'd been measuring. "I've got to know about it now. Are we still going to sell Cirque?"

Daddy stood stock still. "Sell him!" he exclaimed. "What an idea! Cirque can have a golden stall and feed on star dust mixed with diamonds as far as I'm concerned. Perhaps I rushed into things a bit too fast. You seem to be working matters out pretty well in your own way. I'm sorry about the camp, but all the arrangements are made, so I'm afraid you'll have to be a good sport about it this summer."

"Oh, I will, Dad," I vowed. "And I'll promise to enjoy it, if only we don't have to sell Cirque."

He dropped the armful of wood by the stove and went back for another. Then I did the silliest thing. I was so glad inside—too glad for words, I guess. I just cried and cried.

Wake doesn't know I cried, though. He has often told me since that he thinks I was very brave about everything. I'd rather not let him know I cried, because I'd like him to go on thinking that.

June Hall Mills

Sundance

"Take it easy, fella, take it easy," Lissa murmured under her breath, as she watched the two men trying to load the big gelding into the trailer. The horse would not be forced up the ramp. Bright bay hide glistening with sweat, he was fighting, inch by inexorable inch. Foam flecked his mouth and his eyes rolled in desperation. Suddenly panic-stricken, he reared, striking blindly with his front hoofs.

Caught off guard, the bull-necked handler cursed. His wizened partner mumbled, "Fool hoss acts plum loco."

Fear, like the brush of a hawk's wing, shadowed Lissa's face. What if they hurt her horse? What if they hurt Sundance? He meant so much to her. He had taken the place of all those foolish trifles dear to the heart of every girl—bright scarves, shimmering gowns, jangling charm bracelets—in the shop windows of the town. Lissa had not yearned for these, the unattainable.

Fifteen, freckled and wind-blown, she had known contentment. Riding Sundance, the world was hers. Hers the bitter taste of alkali dust and the harsh glitter of sun in a parched land; a fleeting glimpse of a wildcat, green eyes eloquent with hate; the lonely, stirring cry of coyotes; the blessed smell of rain, foretelling the brief glory of rose and ivory cactus blooming in careless rapture; the pungent tang of pine needles, chewed in contemplation; and the sweet, sad cooing of mourning doves.

Lissa, heeding each whisper of wind among the jack pines, sensing every mood of the Montana foothills, loved the bleak land as only the young can love. Not until this day of the auction had she really been aware of another world beyond the boundaries of sagging fence posts. Now, conscious of her faded jeans and scuffed boots, she stood to one side of the crowd, watching every move of the handlers and each response of her horse.

Sundance, companion and guide, knew every turn in the trail from Bull Mountain to Pompey's Pillar; knew the bone-breaking treachery of prairie-dog holes, the sudden danger of a coiled rattler, the deceptive drop of winding coulees.

But now there would be no more long rides for Lissa. Jeb Owen, her father, convinced at last that this land should never have known the sharp thrust of a plow, was selling the old homestead to a big sheep company. Dry-land farming had become too uncertain. The Owens were moving to town. Jamie could take his dog; the twins, their dolls; Fay would have her hen. But—who knew more surely than Lissa herself?—there would be no place for Sundance.

"How can you stand it?" cried Fay, impulsively linking her arm through Lissa's. "I'd grab Sundance and head for the rims and just let 'em try to find us!"

"You know Pa feels bad enough about selling him."

"All the same, it makes me so blamed mad! And another thing: Why can't you be nice to

Ted Matlock? He's been helping move furniture all morning, and twice I saw him go out of his way to talk to you."

"Well, I . . ."

"You barely said enough to be polite. Don't you like him anymore? I wish I were fifteen. *I* wouldn't snub him."

Lissa sighed but she could not explain. She did not know herself why she was avoiding Ted. He had come from town every summer to visit at the neighboring ranch that belonged to his uncle. In previous years, they had shared lunches, explored trails, and laughed together at their extravagant dreams of the future. This summer for the first time Lissa was aware of Ted's casual, polished assurance and his well-cut clothes, compared to her own stumbling ways, shabby jeans, and made-over shirts.

Maybe it was a part of growing up, this strange shyness and confusion. Only this morning Ted had told her, "Don't feel too bad about Sundance, Lis; I've been wanting—"

"It's all right," she had mumbled, turning away, suddenly ashamed to let him see the depth of her feeling.

Now a frightened snort brought her full attention back to Sundance. He had lunged at the handlers, and now stood trembling.

"Mebbe if we roped him and got another horse alongside to drag him in," suggested the small man.

"I'll lambast him to raw meat first!" exploded the other in sudden vehemence, his eyes on a rusty length of chain lying in the dust.

Lissa thrust Fay aside and snatched the chain. Lips parted, eyes flashing, she warned, "Don't you dare touch my horse!"

There was a long moment of quivering silence, then—"Well, well, a she-wildcat," roared the big wrangler, anger dissolving into mirth, "or a pint-sized mountain lion."

The crowd burst into hearty laughter. Embarrassed but adamant, Lissa faced the men.

"All right, boys," called a deep, clear voice, "let the horse stand!" Brad Matlock, Ted's uncle, came up to Lissa. "My apologies, Miss Owen. But since I made the highest bid, Sundance is my property."

Lissa looked up at him, starched white shirt, gleaming black boots, face as impassive as stone.

"I . . . I reckon he does belong to you now, sir," she admitted in a low voice, "but I would like to make a bargain—I mean, a deal."

"A deal? But I have the bill of sale."

"Not about buying him back. Not about money," she hurried to explain. "Fay, go get Pa!"

Jeb Owen came quickly, his hands still grease-stained from the repair job he had done on the truck. With gentle reproach, he asked, "What's this, Lissa, about you making a deal?"

"Please, Pa. I want to load Sundance into that trailer."

"But Mr. Matlock has his own men—"

"Huh!" snorted Fay. "Those two!"

"I can't bear the way they handle Sundance," Lissa pleaded.

"Lis, do you remember when that pinto broke Mark Hall's leg, trying to kick a way out of the corral chute?"

Lissa nodded.

"Don't you savvy . . ." He paused, then glanced at her stricken face and capitulated. "Maybe I'm all kinds of a fool, Mr. Matlock, but I would be much obliged if you would give my daughter a chance to see what she can do."

Brad Matlock nodded. "Miss Owen, the arena is yours."

Lissa gave her father a quick hug, then hurried to the creek for a pail of water and stopped at the barn for a currycomb.

Overhead a hawk hung anchored in the sky. The atmosphere had grown tense and heavy. Even the crowd was subdued. In spite of herself, Lissa looked for Ted and was surprised by her relief at seeing him close to the trailer.

She went up to the lathered horse and spoke to him quietly, permitted him a nuzzling of water. Then she began to curry him, talking to him soothingly in a low voice. The gelding flicked his ears with interest. Untying the halter, she swung herself up on his back, caressing him with her voice, daring to touch his flanks.

Then she urged him forward. He placed one foot upon the ramp. Lissa felt his tremor of fear. Dismounting, she rubbed his leg, smoothed his flank, murmuring gently.

Again and again, she started the horse forward. Many times he faltered. But at last the weary animal stood in the trailer. Lissa slipped out and was locking the end gate when Sundance whinnied, arching his neck to look for her.

She fumbled for the latch through a blur of tears. Then a steady hand guided her trembling fingers, and the gate clicked with finality. She looked up to see Ted beside her.

She heard the long sigh of relief that came from the crowd, Fay's squeal of delight, her father's proud, "Best horse wrangler in Yellowstone County!"

All at once, Lissa was very tired. As she picked up the pail and the currycomb, she felt a hand on her shoulder and, half expecting it to be Ted, was surprised to see Brad Matlock.

"I've seen a lot of horsemen, child," he said, "but only a few with the true understanding of horseflesh. You have the gift. Never forget it."

A look of understanding passed between them. "I'll remember, sir," Lissa said.

"Sundance and his owner will welcome you to the ranch as often as you can come," Brad Matlock said. His eyes were twinkling, as he turned away.

Ted reached for the pail and currycomb. "There's something I've been trying to tell you," he said. "Uncle Brad didn't buy Sundance for himself. He's giving him to me. Says I can work for him summertimes, fixing fences, hunting

strays, things like that. You don't have to worry, Lis; I'll take good care of your horse for you."

It was a moment before Lissa was able to speak. What a fool she had been to worry about her clothes, her lack of sophistication. What did such things matter between friends? She faced Ted squarely. "I've been all mixed up, Ted," she said. "I got to thinking . . . you know, I never did care about fancy clothes and it didn't matter, out here in the hills. But in town the girls are so smooth and dress so well. I don't know anyone from town, except you. I was afraid you might be sort of . . . ashamed of me."

"Lis, are you ever nuts!" He burst out in evident relief. "I didn't know what was wrong—the upstage way you were treating me. You heard what Uncle Brad said about Sundance and his owner wanting you to visit the ranch. If your folks will have me, I can ride down once in a while weekends. You can visit with Sundance, and I can show you around town."

Heedless of the crowd, they walked slowly back to the barn. Lissa thought she had never seen the sky so blue.

Frances Priddy

Palomino Cupid

I ask you, what would you do if you woke up to find yourself in a perfectly strange room, with a horse staring in the window at you, with daisies in its mouth?

I'll tell you what *I* did—I blinked three times and made a wild grab for my glasses. By the time I had finished blinking, I remembered that I was at Aunt Jo's cottage on Lake Alpine, and the room was strange to me because I had arrived on the midnight train and my cousin Linda and I had gone to bed without turning on the light.

With my glasses on, the horse still looked like a horse—a palomino—eating daisies. I mention this because, without glasses, I once mistook a big box for a cow—not what you call 20–20 vision! But I was no closer to knowing why the horse was there, or why the daisies. What a kooky thing to see when you first wake up.

Linda was still sound asleep in the other twin bed, so I figured she wouldn't mind if I borrowed her shirt and shorts—mine were still packed and I didn't want to take time to dig them out. I pulled on Linda's. They were too big, but with luck they wouldn't fall off. I dashed outside to get a closer look at the horse and maybe find out who owned him. I love to ride, and this palomino was a beauty.

But when I got outdoors, the horse was gone. His white tail was just swishing through a gap in the hedge. But—and a big but—it wasn't alone. A boy was leading it. And what a boy!

He was walking away from me and I couldn't see his face, but even so, I could tell he wasn't just any old boy. He was tall as a basketball player, broad shouldered as a football captain, and the way his blond crew cut looked with the sun shining on it did something to me.

My first thought was to yell, "Hey!" at him and find out where he was going with that horse. Then I remembered how I must look, in Linda's clothes, and with my hair uncombed, and instead of flagging him down I very quietly slipped back into the house and went in to wake Linda.

"*Who* is that perfectly gorgeous man next door, the one who just came to get the horse?" I demanded when Linda was awake enough to listen.

It was her turn to blink. Then frown. "Gol-lee, you mean he's been over here again? Golden Boy. That's the horse, I mean. The fellow's Walt Craig. And you might as well go back to bed, doll."

I stared at her, wondering just for a second if Linda had staked out a claim to Walt Craig, but then I remembered Linda had a steady named Jim Thomas or Thompson.

So I demanded to know what she was talking about. Linda sat up, hugging her knees. "Because Walt cares for no one but that horse, that's why. As far as he's concerned, girls don't exist. Every girl I know has tried to break the news to him that there are boys and *girls*, not just boys and *horses*, but no luck. Pity. He's a dreamboat!"

I went back to bed. I figured I might as well. Linda flopped down, rolled over onto her tummy, and snuggled her face into the pillow.

Then I sat bolt upright. "What'd you mean,

he's been over here *again?* How often does he come over? The horse, that is."

Linda un-snuggled, and heaved a sigh. "Lots oftener than Walt, believe me! A couple of times a day, as a rule. He knows how to open his pasture gate. Walt doesn't know how he does it, so Walt can't stop him. But Walt had better learn soon because Golden Boy has eaten most of Mom's flowers."

I nodded and lay down again, but unlike Linda, not to sleep. I was making plans. What girl wants to sleep when she can make plans—especially when those plans revolve around a dreamboat with a golden crew cut?

When we got up, you can bet I put on my cutest shorts and top, and did my hair three times before it suited me. But while we were eating breakfast, I spotted Walt backing out the family car, and taking off. Well, things could have been worse. He'd have to come back sooner or later.

Golden Boy was in his pasture when I went out, and was he a beauty! His coat was a bright rich gold with a satiny sheen, his mane and tail were like ivory silk, and he had just the right amount of white markings. For a moment, I forgot about his owner and just drooled over that horse!

He was friendly, too—came right over when I called, and let me pet him and feed him an apple I had cut up in bite-size pieces. He liked that even better than Aunt Jo's daisies. By the time we finished that apple, Golden Boy was following me all up and down the length of the pasture fence. What a honey! I wondered if I could coax Walt into letting me ride Golden Boy sometime. I had more than one reason now for wanting to know Walt!

Linda and I were sunbathing on the beach when Walt came back. I got my first good look at him then, and WOW! He was even better-looking from the front! He had a widow's peak hairline, alert blue eyes, and a cleft in his chin calculated to make any girl do flips.

Linda reached over and patted my shoulder, sliding a bit because I had just slathered on sun-tan lotion. "Come back," she said patiently. "Come back, doll. As I was saying, this beach party we're having tonight. You'll meet all the crowd then, and—"

"Walt, too?" I asked hopefully. Butterflies were doing the twist in my stomach. I wasn't sure whether it was because of Walt, or the idea of meeting everyone. Ordinarily I'm not shy, but the thought of meeting Linda's crowd en masse made my butterflies step it up, and of course seeing Walt hadn't calmed them! But he would be a familiar face, if he did come to the beach party.

"He's not likely to, so make the best of it," Linda advised. "There are other cute boys around. Not *as* cute, maybe, but available, and that counts for a lot."

She might be right, but I had never encountered any other boy who could make my tummy turn into a dance floor for butterflies, and I was going to get acquainted with Walt Craig or kill myself trying.

I spent the afternoon keeping my eye on Golden Boy's pasture, and before long it paid off. He came trotting around the corner of the fence, tossing his head and looking pleased with himself, making a beeline for Aunt Jo's flowers. Walt spotted him and dashed out to catch him. It was time for me to make my move.

"Hey, there!" I called, running to head off Golden Boy. I hoped Golden Boy hadn't forgotten that apple I had fed him earlier, and thank goodness, he hadn't. He swerved to make straight for me, his ears pricked forward hopefully. When he reached me, he was so busy frisking my pockets to see if I had any apples that I could hardly grab his halter.

"Your horse?" I inquired as Walt joined us. By some miracle, my voice sounded perfectly cool and calm. "He's nice."

"He likes you," Walt commented approvingly, reaching for the halter.

Golden Boy remembered another pocket to investigate just in time to keep Walt from taking the halter from me. He was some horse and that apple had certainly been a good investment.

"Oh, he knows I like him," I said casually. "I get along well with animals. I'm the first person the neighbors think of whenever a cat gets up a tree and won't come down."

"No kidding? So am I in our neighborhood." This time, Walt managed to get hold of Golden Boy's halter.

I still held on, stroking Golden Boy's velvety nose with my free hand, and smoothing his forelock. "Say, I'll bet you'd be just the person to ask!" I said.

"Ask what?" he inquired warily.

"Well—you ride. Obviously." I gave the horse another pat. "So you can tell me, can't you, where I could rent a horse while I'm here? Back home I ride several times a week, and I hate to miss out on it."

Walt nodded, his eyes squinted thoughtfully. "This is swell riding country, too. Well, there's the Lakeview Riding Academy. They have good horses and don't charge too much, either."

He started to give directions, but I couldn't follow them, and said so. "Getting lost is a specialty of mine—along with getting cats down out of trees—and I know I'd never get there, here where I don't know any of the roads or landmarks. I don't suppose—oh, no. I can't bother you."

"What is it?" he asked. "You can try. After all, I can always say no." He gave me a friendly grin that started my butterflies off again.

"To go with me the first time, so I'll know how to get to the stable and back?" I asked hopefully. "And learn the good paths to follow? I'd be awfully grateful—but if you'd rather not—"

"I guess I could," he said, nodding slowly. "Golly. I don't know which paths to tell you. There are so many good ones around here. The Pine Ridge trail, and Hawthorne, and Possum Mountain, and—"

"Stop! You'll confuse me!" I implored. "Listen, I've got an idea. You'll be at the beach party tonight, won't you? Maybe you could tell me about the different paths then, and we could decide."

Walt looked dubious. "Well—I hadn't planned on going. I—"

"Oh, dear!" I said. "I don't know any of Linda's crowd, and the very thought of not knowing a soul—well, it's too much! I need some moral support, believe me! I wish you were coming so there would be at least one familiar face. I have stage fright, but good! And we could talk about the different bridle paths."

"Well—" Walt said again, then grinned. "Well, I'm not much for parties, but I guess I could come and hang around to give you moral support." He was not only a dreamboat, he was sweet, too! "Sure. To tell you the truth, one reason I'm not much for that sort of stuff is that I don't know many of the kids either. Not well, I mean. So we can give each other moral support, okay?"

"Okay," I agreed with heartfelt gratitude, thanking heaven for that gatecrashing, apple-eating palomino cupid. "Okay! See you tonight!"

After that, I could hardly wait for the beach party. Linda said I had done the impossible, and I was so set up that I forgot about feeling quivery over meeting Linda's crowd all at once. When I met them, I wondered why I had ever felt that way, for they were a swell bunch, and I knew we would have a ball.

The beach party was a swinging affair, and I was having the time of my life. When Walt wasn't the first to arrive, I was sort of disappointed, for I had had the impression he would be right there, at my side, all evening; but when he didn't come —and didn't come—I became more and more upset. Linda kept giving me little questioning looks, and I felt like crawling into a hole and pulling it in after me. I wondered if Linda had told her friends, and if they were feeling sorry for me, or worse yet, if they thought I had made up the story that Walt was coming to the party with me. The food, which had seemed so good, turned tasteless for me, and the party fun just seemed noisy and horribly silly.

All of a sudden I couldn't stand it a second longer. I managed to slip away to wander along the beach, trying to figure it out. Why hadn't Walt come, after he had promised? Had he agreed just to get rid of me? I couldn't believe that, not when I remembered the way he had looked, and the way he had smiled at me, his eyes crinkling, when he promised to come. It *couldn't* have been a brush-off—yet what other explanation was there? I didn't want to believe it, but I had to. Maybe I was getting what I had asked for—maybe I shouldn't have bribed Golden Boy with that apple, just to get in good with Walt. But I would have been crazy about that horse even if his owner had been old and ugly! If only I could make Walt understand that.

I stopped and fumbled for my hankie. My eyes were so full of tears that I couldn't see where I was going. Then something crashed through the bushes practically beside me—and gave a queer, high scream!

I screamed, too, then gasped with relief as I realized it hadn't been a scream, just a horse whinnying. A horse? In the woods? At night?

It was pitch dark. I fought my way through the bushes till I bumped right into the horse. I couldn't really see it, but from the way it began nosing my pockets, I knew it was Golden Boy. I felt my way to his head, took hold of his halter, and pulled, but there was a rope clipped to it, and the rope seemed to be fastened to something. I groped my way along it, wishing I had a flashlight so I could see what I was doing. The rope was long, and all tangled up in the bushes. I untangled a couple of feet, with Golden Boy breathing down my neck, trying to help. Finally I gave up and unsnapped the rope from his halter.

The moon came out about that time, and I could see well enough to find a path. I started back to Craigs' cottage, leading Golden Boy. For once, he was glad to go home.

"Golden Boy?" a voice called from around a bend in the path. I recognized it as Walt's. He sounded tired and worried.

"Here he is," I called back. "His rope was all tangled up in the brush down at the shore."

"Golden Boy!" Walt exclaimed, relieved and happy, as he ran to his horse. "Is he okay?"

"He isn't limping," I answered. "It's too dark to really examine him, but I think he's all right."

Walt smiled at me as we left the woods. "I'm sorry I didn't show up," he said. "I staked Golden Boy out so he wouldn't run away again. Then when I went to put him in the stable, he was gone! I guess I didn't pound the stake in deep enough, and he pulled it up. Usually he stays near by; just goes over to eat the neighbors' flowers or something, but tonight he simply vanished! I've been hunting for him ever since. I guess I should have come over to tell you why I was held up, but I thought I'd find him any minute and could make it anyway. I haven't taken time to eat, or anything."

"I wondered where you were, of course," I said slowly, "but after I found him, I had a hunch you were out looking for him. Why don't you put him in his stable and make sure he's okay, then come eat? The party's still in full swing, and there's plenty of food left."

Walt grinned down at me, his eyes crinkling, and reached for my hand. "I'll do that," he promised. "Come with me to put Boy away, then we'll go back to the party together." He gave me another smile, which made me breathe as if I'd been running. "You know, you're not like other girls. Some of them have made quite a fuss over Boy, pretending to be crazy about him, but it was easy to tell they were just faking and didn't know or even like horses. Golden Boy could tell that. He could tell that you were for real, too. Pretty good judge of character, this horse of mine!"

I looked at Golden Boy, glad he had fended off those other girls and that he liked me. And you know what? That horse winked at me—I swear it!

Ellsworth Newcomb

Two for the Show

"Take it easy, boy." Millie Taylor reined her horse in firmly, but she sympathized with his impatience. She wanted to hurry, too. For weeks she had been counting the days till the horse show, and once they reached the club grounds tomorrow's red-letter event would seem that much nearer.

But Mr. Bones must have time to cool off before he was stabled. Millie stroked his brown silk neck; then her heart thudded as she glimpsed the club's white fences. Suddenly she felt panicky. Under the faded dungarees she was wearing, so as to save her one and only pair of jodhpurs for the show, her knees felt wobbly. What if her mother and father were right in thinking that she'd be laughed at for showing Mr. Bones? It was true that, unlike the other girls' mounts, he was a retired Army horse, and didn't have quite their style and perfection. But he could still go like the wind, and Millie had never seen a fence he wouldn't jump. Sleekly groomed as he was now by her loving hands, she was sure anyone would be proud of him, and she simply couldn't miss this chance.

To Millie, the idea of riding in a real horse show was the most thrilling thing in the world. She had dreamed of it for years and had a scrapbook bulging with clippings about famous exhibits. When it had been decided to have a show right here in West Harbor, with a special class for junior misses, she had been dizzy with excitement. It was the most terrific thing that had happened since the day her father had brought Mr. Bones home, six years ago, when Millie was eight.

She had loved Mr. Bones at first sight, and never could get enough of her father's stories about her horse's adventurous days with the squadron, when he had jumped the highest hurdles and been ridden in polo matches and even in sham battles. She had fed him, and groomed him, and nursed him when he had gone lame.

At the beach one afternoon she had heard the older girls talking about the horse show and the classes for junior misses. There were to be three events—horsemanship, a stunt race, and best of all, a jumping class. Any girl from fourteen to sixteen could enter, provided she showed in all three events. Millie had rushed home to tell her mother.

"I'll pay the entrance fee out of my allowance," she finished in haste, remembering she had heard quite a lot of talk about expenses lately.

"But Millicent Taylor," her mother said, frowning, "you certainly can't be serious. We all love Mr. Bones, but he isn't a show horse. Lucy Trent will be exhibiting one of their prize winners, and all the other girls have show horses. Why, you'd be laughed out of the ring."

Her father, who had been so touchy and worried all summer, was even more out of patience. "I'm sick and tired of all this horse talk," he declared. "I should have sold Mr. Bones long ago. He's a needless expense when we should be cutting down."

Millie's blue eyes were dark with tears as she

started for the door, determined not to let her parents see her cry. Then all at once her father relented.

"Oh, all right," he said. "If it means that much to you, go ahead. But I think you'll be sorry."

Millie headed for the barn to feed Mr. Bones.

"If only we could have afforded to send her to camp," she heard her mother sigh.

"If I could land that Trent account a lot of things would be possible," her father's voice drifted out to her. "But I can't seem to get the man to see me."

Millie puzzled over the scrap of conversation for a moment. She knew Mr. Trent was the head of a big manufacturing company and her father was with an advertising agency. Probably the agency would like to handle the Trent Company advertising. But she had far too many dazzling plans for the show whirling around in her head to leave room for grownups' problems.

Two weeks after that she had felt very important when she paid her entrance fee and was given the round white tag with EXHIBITOR printed on it. The tag was now fastened to the top button of her crumpled blouse, and as she turned into the Hunt Club drive she watched it swing in time to Mr. Bones's steps, and all her excitement over tomorrow's show flooded back.

"We'll win a prize, won't we, boy?" she whispered as they neared the long, low stables beyond which, circled by green lawns, the club-house lifted its graceful white columns.

"Hi there, Millie!" A girl in trim jodhpurs greeted her from the back of a handsome roan whose bridle was being adjusted by one of the club grooms. "What are you doing so far from home?"

Before Millie could answer, half a dozen girls in expensively correct riding habits swarmed up, and her heart sank as she saw Lois Deane's mocking eyes squint at her from a surrounding network of freckles. At school Lois made the lives of the younger girls miserable with her teasing, but surely here, where they were all on an equal footing, she'd be decent.

Lois, however, had no such ideas of good sportsmanship. "Don't look now," she said loudly, "but that's an exhibitor's tag Millie's wearing along with those priceless dungarees. Friends, I do believe she's entered that Army nag of hers in the junior-miss classes. We'd better watch our steps."

When peals of laughter broke around her, Millie felt exactly the way she had the day the baseball hit her in the pit of the stomach. All these girls were older than she, but most of them went to her school and she had often ridden with them. Except for Lois, she thought of them as friends. Yet here in the formal, manicured grounds of the club—to which the Taylors did not belong—they were ready to follow Lois in making fun of her old clothes and of Mr. Bones. As if she hadn't just as much right to show her horse as anyone!

She rallied after a stunned moment. "Of course I'm riding Mr. Bones tomorrow. What's wrong with that?"

"Oh, not a thing in the world," squealed Lois. "I only wish all the horses were like him. Then I'd be *sure* of winning."

Her face crimson, Millie dismounted quickly and led Mr. Bones to the stall he was to occupy. Her hands shook as she unsaddled him. How right her mother and father had been! The girls did think it was a huge joke to show Mr. Bones. If today was this bad, tomorrow would be a nightmare. For a miserable second she hid her dust-streaked cheek against her horse's smooth neck and longed to go home. But that would be admitting she was ashamed. Ashamed of dear, gentle Mr. Bones! Her chin came up, high and determined. No matter what the girls said, she wouldn't back down now.

Ignoring them all, she was busily applying saddle soap to her tack when a horse van rumbled into the drive, followed by Lucy Trent's smart convertible.

The Trents owned the biggest place in West Harbor and showed their famous horses all over the country. Lucy had even ridden at Madison Square Garden in New York. If Lois, whose horse was really nothing to brag about, thought Millie was crazy to have entered Mr. Bones, what on earth would Lucy say?

Millie concentrated on rubbing a sweat stain out of her saddle as Lucy joined the group of girls. They all watched her bay mare being led out of the luxurious van, then exclaimed when a second horse, a fine black gelding, followed.

"Well, for Pete's sake," Lois asked tartly, "what's the idea of bringing *two* horses to the show?"

Lucy laughed. "Dad insisted on entering Pride. He hopes I'll change my mind and ride him instead of Blarney. But I think I'll stick to the one I'm used to, though of course Pride is the best jumper in our stable."

"Relax," said Lois, a malicious grin dividing her freckles. "Millie Taylor is showing Old Bones —or whatever his name is. So none of us has a chance, no matter what horse we decide we want to ride."

Lucy's gray eyes found Millie. "Oh, hi." She smiled in a friendly fashion. "I didn't see you. Don't you want a stableboy to do that scrubbing for you?"

"No, thanks." Millie clenched her teeth. Lucy was the nicest older girl she knew, and probably meant the suggestion kindly. But it did call attention to the fact that Millie was the only one who took care of her own tack. Even for this big event her allowance wouldn't cover club service.

"Ugh." Lois glanced at her fingernails. "I'd hate that messy job, wouldn't you, Lucy?"

Lucy gave her a stony look. "I'd be proud if I could take care of my horse and tack as well as Millie does," she said.

Millie felt her heart swell with gratitude, but Lucy's championship only seemed to egg Lois on, and when, later, they all took their horses out for a trial canter around the ring, she renewed her attack.

"It's a cinch Millie will never fall off that sway-back," she remarked.

Lucy quietly edged her beautiful mare over beside Millie. "Lois is just showing off," she said. "She's pea-green with jealousy because she knows you're a better rider than any of us. There's not a thing wrong with Mr. Bones. He's just a little rounder and plumper than the others."

Millie willed back her tears. Lucy was comforting, but even though she'd rather have Mr. Bones than any show horse alive, she had to admit that he did lack some of the points for which a judge would look.

"I've always wanted to ride in a show," she confessed shakily.

"Millie!" Lucy was suddenly on fire with excitement. "I'd love to see you teach Lois a lesson. I've had a brain wave. Not only are you going to ride in the show tomorrow—you're going to win! You can ride Pride. He's won dozens of prizes and Dad says he's the best horse in the state."

Pride! For a delirious moment Millie pictured herself astride that magnificent black horse—all eyes focused on her as she pranced into the ring. Everyone applauding as she was awarded the trophy. What a chance to make her family proud of her!

But that would be a horrid thing to do to Mr. Bones. She wasn't going to desert him just because a stupid girl had made fun of him. She shook her head. "You're swell, Lucy," she said, "but no, thanks. I wouldn't feel right about Mr. Bones."

Back at the stables, she was relieved to find her mother waiting to drive her home.

"You look sick," Mrs. Taylor told her. "Really, darling, I wish you wouldn't insist on going through with this."

Goodness, what would her mother think if she knew Millie had turned down the chance to ride one of the Trent horses?

By one o'clock the next afternoon the club's parking lot was packed with cars. Busy with her final grooming of Mr. Bones, Millie looked up now and then to watch for her mother and father. When at last she saw them, she felt cold in spite of the intense heat. Suppose all those gaily dressed people should laugh at her, just as Lois had? Her family would be so ashamed they might even tell her she couldn't keep Mr. Bones any longer. They were already annoyed because she had insisted on showing him, and if she humiliated them by making herself ridiculous today it might be the last straw. Yet she couldn't back down now. It was as if Lois, her family, everyone, were daring her to prove what a wonderful horse Mr. Bones was. And she must prove it. She must win!

As if to assure her he would do his best, Mr. Bones whinnied softly and nuzzled her shoulder. Millie gave him a swift pat. Just then Lucy and Mr. Trent arrived, with Lois trailing them.

"My daughter tells me you're quite a horsewoman," Mr. Trent said. "I'd like to have you ride Pride for me. How about it?"

There it was again; the dazzling chance to ride a famous show horse, to make sure of carrying off the prize!

But Millie politely but resolutely again said no to the generous offer.

At once Lois laid a pleading hand on Mr. Trent's arm. "Please, please," she begged, "let me show Pride, Mr. Trent. It would make me the happiest girl in the world."

Millie was sure she saw a look of annoyance

flicker in Mr. Trent's eyes, but it was gone instantly and Lois's face flamed with triumph as he gave his consent.

Lucy and Millie exchanged crestfallen glances. Lois had tipped the scales neatly in her own favor. With Pride as her mount, the jumping-class trophy—the most coveted of the prizes—was as good as hers, and perhaps all the others besides.

But it was time for the first of the junior-miss classes to begin. Mr. Trent held Mr. Bones while Millie swung up into the saddle, and they all started for the ring.

In the noise, heat, and confusion, Millie felt her knees go wobbly again. She dreaded this first event most of all, because not only would riders be judged on horsemanship, but the horses themselves were to score on manners, performance, and conformation, and although she rode well and Mr. Bones obeyed her lightest touch, she knew that he hadn't a chance against the other horses; against Pride's gleaming perfection. In an agony of self-consciousness she circled the ring with the others.

Walk. Trot. Canter. Would it never be over? As long as the rules said you had to enter this class if you entered any, maybe she shouldn't have shown Mr. Bones at all. She could see that the judge wasn't even looking at him. But with Mr. Bones's polo background he still might win the stunt class. She clung to that hope as they finally lined up in front of the judges and the ordeal ended at last, with Lois riding out of the ring with the blue ribbon, while Lucy's mount got second prize, and the third went to Marjie Green's tall roan.

"You'll win something this time," Lucy called encouragingly to Millie while they waited for the signal for the stunt event.

Millie managed a smile. Here was her chance. They were to race their horses to the far side of the ring where a row of "helpers" stood ready to sew a big red button on the sleeve of each rider as she dismounted. The prize would go to the one who first got back with the button in place.

Millie's pulse pounded as the horses sped across the ring. This was Mr. Bones's dish. Now he'd show what he could do. "Go to it, boy," she whispered, and as if he understood, the Army-trained horse sprinted to Millie's helper a nose ahead of the others.

"Hurray!" thought Millie, jumping to the ground and holding out her sleeve, while Mr.

Bones stood like a statue. After what seemed an age, the button was sewed on and Millie was back in the saddle a split second ahead of the other girls. Mr. Bones whirled and raced back neck and neck with Pride. Then suddenly he was ahead—actually at the base an inch ahead of Lois's horse.

Ready to shout for joy, Millie flung up her arm. The button was gone! Evidently too hurriedly stitched, it had fallen off during the race, while Lois's winked brightly on her sleeve as once again she took first prize.

Millie's throat felt thick with tears. Her one chance to win was gone. The next and final event was the jumping class, and Pride could outjump any horse in the show.

"There's no use even trying," she thought miserably. Then she squared her shoulders. Mr. Bones was a fine jumper, and even if he couldn't beat Pride he was entitled to his chance to prove his mettle. She'd finish what she had started.

Feeling as if a blanket of lead were pressing the breath out of her, Millie watched the hurdles being set up. The three-foot bars suddenly looked mountain high. It was no use to remind herself that she had put Mr. Bones over many a fence just as tall. Here, in the heat and confusion, everything seemed different. Mr. Bones's leg might go lame again or, nervous as she was, she might handle him badly. Her family, Lois—even Lucy—expected her to fail, and now her own confidence was gone. Tensely she heard a number called and saw the first horse enter the ring. With a swerve the big hunter almost unseated his rider as he refused the jump. Then Lucy's pretty mare charged forward, ticked a bar, and sent it crashing.

When Millie's number was called, every girl but Lois had had her turn and not a single horse had taken all the hurdles without a fault. If the others couldn't make it, what chance had she? And there sat Lois astride her borrowed horse, smugly confident that she would wind up the show in glory!

As Millie started hopelessly into the ring, something wet spattered her hand and for an awful moment she wondered if it were her own tears. Then she heard the low growl of distant thunder and knew it had begun to rain. The cool drops were like a whiplash on Mr. Bones's flanks, and he was galloping toward the first hurdle when a jagged fork of lightning raked the sky and thunder roared with the deafening sound of a hundred canon. Then rain and noise blotted out the world, and Millie was agonizingly afraid that her horse would bolt. But as she forced herself to lean forward and give Mr. Bones his head, she felt his legs gather under him, as he cleared the hurdle in a beautiful, soaring spring. And now he was over the second. And the third.

Magnificently he finished the course, as if the roar of the sudden storm were nothing but the noise of the sham battles remembered from his Army days. What a warrior he was! Why, if it weren't for Pride, he'd surely win the trophy for that performance.

Shaking rain out of her eyes, Millie saw the crowd of spectators running for shelter in wild confusion. But Lois, ignoring the judge's signal to wait, stubbornly galloped into the ring and headed Pride for the number-one hurdle. He was racing for it with his long, effortless stride when once again a burst of thunder seemed to split the sky apart. Pride stiffened his legs and stopped, frozen with fright. Millie heard her own startled cry as Lois went hurtling over his head. For a horrifying moment Millie thought she must be hurt, but Lois was on her feet before the ring steward could reach her. She wiped mud from her angry face and ran from the ring.

By the time Pride had been caught and quieted, the flash storm was over. Before Millie could realize what was happening, the judge motioned all the contestants back for a line-up. In a spangled daze she watched him head straight for Mr. Bones, then held her breath as he handed her the trophy.

She slid to the ground and flung her arms around Mr. Bones, not caring whether it was rain or tears that blurred her eyes.

"You certainly stuck to the right horse," Lucy beamed delightedly. "I knew Pride would bolt the moment I heard the thunder. He's always been terrified of it."

Out of the crowd around her, Millie heard her father's voice.

"We're mighty proud of you, and Mr. Bones, too." He gave Millie a hug, then turned as Mr. Trent came up to them.

"I like Millie's kind of loyalty," Mr. Trent chuckled as they shook hands. As Millie's father looked puzzled, he told how she had refused his offer of Pride. "For once I actually was delighted to see one of my own horses beaten," he added.

"Say, Taylor, we're having a little after-the-show affair at the house. Won't you and Mrs. Taylor and Millie join us? I think it's high time we got acquainted."

As the girls rode back to the stables, Millie hugged her trophy to make sure she wasn't dreaming. This was the happiest, proudest day of her life. Not only had her horse won a prize in a real show, but now that he had covered himself with glory, there'd be no more talk of selling him.

Outside Mr. Bones's stall, where his blue ribbon was now tacked over the door for everyone to see, Lois awkwardly shook hands with Millie. "Lucky girl," she said stiffly, "to have a horse that isn't scared of storms. You don't suppose he's deaf, do you?"

But Millie felt much too happy to mind. Not even Lois's barbed remarks could bother her now.

Margaret Burrage

A Horse in Her Future

Darlene Manners leaned one shoulder against the wide doors of Barn One and watched wistfully as Hank Cenno, riding master of the 7-Hills Riding Academy, led his pupils on another ride.

"If only I had a horse," Darlene thought longingly, "I could be going with them."

Ever since she could remember Darlene had loved horses. It had begun at the age of two with her first hobbyhorse and progressed to riding her nextdoor neighbor's Shetland pony until her legs grew too long. Now, at fifteen, her love of horses was so deeply ingrained that for some time she had been doing barn chores at the riding academy just for the privilege of handling and exercising the horses. At first Hank had protested from time to time over her working so hard, but now, in his absent-minded way, he had come to depend upon her.

Darlene shifted her shoulders against the rough boards of the barn. Not having a horse was, at the moment, only one of her problems. Overlying her deep wish for a mount all her own was the knowledge that, unless a miracle occurred, next Monday would find her working in a stuffy office. Her heart constricted at the thought. It wasn't that she didn't want to help Dad by earning her own allowance and her school clothes for fall, it was just that she couldn't bear to leave the horses!

It had all started the night before, at dinner. "Money's going to be tight for a while, Chicken Little," her father had told her reluctantly. "I'm branching out into real estate for myself, so instead of a regular salary, I'll be on my own. It won't leave much except for necessities. I'm afraid your allowance . . ."

"That's all right, Dad," Darlene had reassured him quickly. "Perhaps I can find a job."

Both her father and mother had looked relieved. "I was talking with Chuck Wilcox the other day," her father said. "He needs someone to do simple filing at his insurance office. I'll call him if you like. At least that'll save you from job hunting." His voice was husky.

At the look of hurt pride on his face, Darlene tried to act pleased. "That'll be neat, Dad," she said, her voice as gay as she could make it.

Her mother reached across the table and patted her hand. "Personally, I'll be relieved to have you stop playing around that riding club," she said. "Why, you talk, eat, and breathe horses! You have no friends any more. You actually seem to like horses better than you do girls your own age."

Darlene plopped jelly on her bread. "I *do* like them better," she said flatly. "They're not silly; they do what you want them to; and they don't fight with you like that hateful Michele Adams!"

Mrs. Manners looked at her husband and raised her hands in a gesture of despair. "Your mother's right," Bob Manners said. "You do need friends your own age. Perhaps this is for the best."

Darlene's heart constricted now just thinking

of it. How could it be "best"—to be cooped in a stuffy insurance office all summer? I can't do it, she thought in despair. I just can't.

As the gay cavalcade rode past, Hank broke into her thoughts. He turned, straight and tall, in his saddle, raising his riding crop in a little salute. "Watch out for Michele, will you, Darlene? She's practicing out on the track."

Darlene made a wry face. "Okay," she called back in flat resignation.

Ever since they first had met, she and Michele Adams had kept up a running feud. Michele owned the most magnificent of all the quarter horses boarded at the stables, and her tack, studded with glittering silver *conchas*, was expensive, but she was an indifferent rider. Worst of all, she infuriated Darlene by the slipshod manner in which she groomed both her horse and tack.

Darlene could see her now in the distance at the far end of the practice track. She was riding slumped in the saddle instead of with heel, hip, and shoulder in a straight line as Hank taught.

"Doing everything wrong, as usual," Darlene said to herself. "She shouldn't hold Lobo back like that! It's okay on the turns but on the straightaway she should know enough to give him his head."

Hank had worked as hard with Michele as he had with the others. First they had been given classroom work. This consisted of a talk on horses and their reactions and an illustrated lecture on care of equipment—Michele had sure failed that one, Darlene thought wryly—then they were given thorough instruction in saddling up, followed by the do's and don'ts of riding. After that came the actual practice work of saddling and unsaddling, done over and over until it became automatic, and only then came the mounting of their horses.

For the more backward of his pupils, Hank put a saddle on a wooden sawhorse and required them to mount over and over until they could do it with ease. Of course, Michele had been one of these.

That really must have hurt her pride, Darlene thought with sympathy. But it needn't have stopped her from listening to Hank's advice and following it when riding!

At least Michele was in no trouble at the moment. Darlene went back to her barn chores and her depressing thoughts. When a shadow darkened the door, she looked up to see Michele carrying in her saddle. She draped it carelessly across an empty stall door, the saddle blanket dragging on the floor.

"Hi, Darlene," she called in greeting. "Hank tells me you're leaving and going to work in an *office.*" Her voice held a sort of shocked disapproval.

Darlene continued to spread shavings carefully in an even thickness on the floor of the stall. "Maybe I will and maybe I won't," she answered. "I talked with Mr. Miner this morning and he half-promised me a job working evenings at his drugstore. I'll know for sure tonight. If my father will let me take that, I can keep on here days."

"I can't imagine why you want to," Michele said spitefully. "You work like a stableboy and you don't even own a horse!"

"You forget that Hank lets me exercise Gay!" Darlene shot back. The moment she said it, she was sorry. Her own love of horses made her realize that it wasn't fair to remind Michele that Darlene was the only one Hank ever permitted to ride the beautiful but treacherous black mare Michele admired so much.

"I have to check on the horses in the paddock,"

Darlene said quickly, and dashed out of the barn. At the paddock fence, she stopped to catch her breath, her cheeks hot with embarrassment. How could she have said such a mean thing!

Dusty, her favorite of all the stable mounts, mane and tail flowing in the breeze, trotted over to nuzzle her shoulder. She patted his gleaming chestnut coat, admiring him extravagantly.

"Aren't you the beauty, though," she crooned. "You're stacks handsomer than that old Gay!"

As if in answer to her name, Gay separated herself from the other horses and darted toward the paddock fence. Her movements were swift, effortless, and flowing. As she reached the gate she wheeled, and lashing out with both hind feet, kicked viciously at Dusty's sleek flank. With a quick, instinctive maneuver the other horse evaded the flashing hooves.

"Shame on you," Darlene scolded, admiring in spite of herself the spirited small mare with her slender legs, muscular neck, and deep chest. "How can you look so beautiful and be so mean?"

Gay put her ears back, snaked her slender neck forward, and nickered loudly. Darlene gave both horses an extra pat and went back into the barn. Michele was gone.

From the last stall, Lobo whinnied softly. Darlene hurried to him down the cool, dark aisle. Lather coated his flanks and his neck was wet. Anger exploded in Darlene's chest. That Michele! She had done it again! She had put Lobo in his stall without bothering to cool him off.

If that isn't just like her, Darlene fumed to herself. She knows I'll walk Lobo for her rather than let him get all stiffened up. As soon as she had finished with Lobo, Darlene hurried to complete her regular chores. When Hank returned with his group of riders, she was nearly through for the night.

The young people tended their mounts, then raced for the clubhouse to buy snacks. Darlene watched them wistfully. What fun it must be to go on a real trail ride instead of just exercising horses alone. She gave herself a small shake. What was she complaining about? She was lucky to have this chance to work with horses at all. At least, she was with them for today, anyway. All the gloomy thoughts she had been keeping in the back of her mind returned in a dismal cloud. What if she couldn't persuade her father to let her take that job at Miner's Drug Store? What if she had to work in an office all day and never have a chance to ride or be with horses at all?

"I can't bear to leave," she thought desperately. "I just can't!"

She dropped her now empty water pail and threw both arms around Belafonte, the golden palomino she had just watered. "Oh, Bella," she cried, her voice choked with tears, "how could I ever leave and never see you again? You and Dusty and the others?"

Behind her Hank entered the dim barn. "Almost through for the night?" he asked cheerfully.

Darlene kept her back turned while she hastily dabbed at her eyes. "Hi, Hank," she said steadily. "Have a good trail ride?"

"So-so," Hank answered. "Most of the class is catching on pretty well. Not one is a natural like you, though!" His face lighted. "What a way you have with horses! Why, with you even Gay almost behaves."

"I wouldn't say that exactly," Darlene said dryly. "I have to master her every minute."

"I said almost, didn't I?" Hank laughed. Then his face sobered and he laid his hand lightly on Darlene's shoulder. "I know how you feel about leaving the stables, Funnyface," he said. "But it's a strange thing about something you really want to do. If you want it bad enough, you can always find a way."

"I hope that's true," Darlene said fervently. "I hope somehow I can find a way." Later, as she walked slowly along toward Miner's Drug Store she kept on hoping it with all of her heart.

Mr. Miner stepped from behind the counter as soon as he saw Darlene. "Came about the job, didn't you? I'm awful sorry, Miss Manners," he said regretfully, "but my wife's nephew took it. I couldn't help myself. My wife—well—you know how it is."

He was so obviously distressed that Darlene hastened to reassure him. "It's all right, Mr. Miner," she said. "I'm sure I can find something else."

"Hope you do." Mr. Miner's round face puckered with concern. "Sure hope you do. You know that."

"Thank you." Darlene left quickly, swallowing desperately at the lump that was beginning to form in her throat. She mustn't cry here on the street. Safe at home in her own room, however, she buried her face deep in her pillow and let the sobs come.

Next morning Hank met her at the barn door. There was a worried pucker on his forehead. "Listen, Funnyface," he said hurriedly, "I'll have to ask you to exercise three of the horses this afternoon. Think you can squeeze in all that riding after the barn chores?"

Ordinarily, Darlene would have been overjoyed at such an opportunity, but today she was too discouraged to show any enthusiasm. "Yes, of course I'll do it, Hank," she answered soberly.

Hank tapped beneath her jaw lightly with one forefinger. "Hey, chin up there!" he smiled. "Remember what I told you. There's always a way." He set off quickly for the clubhouse.

Darlene's jaw tightened. "Sure there's always a way," she told herself, "and I just won't let one setback discourage me. I'll find some way, wait and see!"

Today when the riding club members left on their trail ride, Darlene, thinking of the three horses she had to exercise, felt only a momentary pang of envy. From the corner of her eye she saw Michele listlessly riding Lobo on the now empty practice track.

"Why, it must be hard for her, too, to see the

trail riders go out," Darlene realized suddenly. "If only she'd try harder she'd be able to ride well enough to go along."

By mid-afternoon the barn chores were done. "Now to exercise those horses," she thought with satisfaction. Unlocking the tackroom, she filled her pockets with carrots. As she crossed the wide area to the paddock, Dusty came sweeping up to the gate, nose extended. She fed him a carrot. The other horses crowded about the fence, too, and she fed them all, petting each in turn.

"Funny Gay isn't right in the front row," she thought in surprise. "I think I'll exercise her first, while my hands and wrists aren't tired."

Carefully she searched, looking over the horses one by one, but she saw no star-faced black mare. There was no doubt about it, Gay was gone. "That rascal," she thought in exasperation. "Now how could she ever have jumped the fence?" Then from out on the track she heard the thundering sound of hooves.

Whirling about she saw Gay, ears tight against her head, her body stretched low—and on her back, obviously already in danger of losing her seat, was Michele!

For one moment Darlene stood frozen, her

hands pressed against her mouth. Then she sprang into action. Dusty! There was no time for a saddle. Springing up on his bare back, she clutched his halter. With a flying start the chestnut was off up the track. Guiding him by knee pressure alone, Darlene bent low over his neck. Ahead of her Gay stretched out as if flying. Despite the danger of the moment, Darlene felt a thrill of admiration for the black tornado.

"Stretch yourself, Dusty," she urged, "or you'll never catch her!"

Dusty put on another spurt of speed. He had found his stride now, and the pines at the far side of the track passed in a blur. Michele had lost her stirrups and was clinging desperately to the saddle as she bounced about.

If only she can hang on, Darlene thought. She urged Dusty onward. Michele will fall—she'll be killed—faster, Dusty, faster! With a surge Dusty reached the mare's flank. For what seemed years to Darlene they stayed there, not gaining, not losing. Then they began to creep up.

If only Michele doesn't panic—if only I'm strong enough! As they drew up beside the black mare, Darlene reached out and grasped Michele about the waist. Michele grabbed her shoulder, almost unseating her. Then Michele was free of the saddle.

Dusty slowed to a smooth, even stop. Darlene let Michele drop lightly to the ground. Ahead of them, Gay stopped too and began nibbling unconcernedly at the grass in the center of the track.

"You all right, Michele?" Darlene asked shakily.

Michele's face was subdued and white. "I—I guess so."

"Then you lead Dusty while I catch Gay."

When Darlene returned with the black mare, Michele was plodding along the track leading Dusty. Something about the droop of her shoulders touched Darlene.

"Go ahead and say it," Michele said. "I had no business taking Gay and I'll never make a rider."

Darlene tried for a light touch. "You'll never *live* to make a rider if you try Gay again! Until you've ridden a lot more, that is. I've got a good knee grip and strong hands, but that horse gives me plenty of trouble."

Michele's shoulders drooped even lower. "Let's face it," she said. "I can't even ride Lobo, let

alone any other horse. I'd better sell him and just give up trying to ride."

Darlene laughed. "You give up?" she said. "A girl with nerve enough to tackle a horse like Gay? You know you won't do that. Listen, I'm supposed to exercise Paint, Rebel, and Gay today. I guess Gay's already had her share of exercise, so how about your riding Lobo while I exercise the others?"

For the remainder of the afternoon the two girls rode together, Darlene patiently coaching and directing. When Hank returned with the Trail Riders, Darlene showed off her pupil's progress. Hank was delighted. "You're doing just fine, Michele," he beamed. "You're really getting the feel of your mount now. Say, we'll have you on trail ride in no time!"

"You know something, Darlene?" Michele said when Hank had left for the clubhouse, "That's the first time he ever praised me. Listen, when I can ride well enough, will you take one of the track horses and ride the trail with me?"

At the look on Darlene's face her voice faltered and stopped. "Oh, Darlene, didn't you—you mean you didn't get the drugstore job?"

"Mr. Miner gave the job to his wife's nephew," Darlene said flatly.

"Oh, Darlene, what will you do now? Why, you can't give up coming to the academy. Not now when we can have so much fun riding together!"

Darlene squared her shoulders. "I'll find some way," she said, trying to sound confident. But the confidence was all in her voice. What was there that she could do now? Monday was only one more day away.

Later, alone in the barn, she fed and watered the horses. The day, and perhaps her work at the stables, too, was at an end. She was tired. "Not that I mind being tired," she told herself quickly. "Not when I get tired doing what I like to do—even if I *don't* get paid for it," she added ruefully.

A sudden thought struck her and she made some rapid mental calculations. I do believe it would work, she thought slowly. Yes, it would—I'll bet it would. *Yippee!* She threw the oat measure she was holding high up into the air and caught it. Then she sought out Hank.

"Hank, may I talk with you?" she asked. "It's business and it's important."

An hour later, Darlene raced home and burst

into the living room where her father was reading the paper.

"Dad," she said breathlessly, "what would Mr. Wilcox pay me at the office?"

Her father laid down his paper and picked up his pipe. "Oh, about ten dollars a week, I guess."

Darlene took a deep breath. "Dad, I can earn twice that at the 7-Hills Riding Academy. Now, wait, Dad—hear me through before you say anything." Swiftly she outlined all the barn chores that she had been doing at the track. "And," she went on, "all of a sudden I decided that no matter how much I enjoy doing those chores, they're worth good hard cash. For just a minute," she chuckled, "I was afraid Hank didn't feel that way, but he was so embarrassed because he hadn't thought of paying me himself that he's going to pay me a lump sum for the work I've done these past weeks. Isn't that super?"

Her father puffed thoughtfully on his pipe. "And what do you plan to do with all that wealth?"

"I've got it all figured out," Darlene said promptly. "The back pay goes into my college fund and so does five dollars a week. Five dollars will go towards school clothes for fall. The rest I'd . . . I'd sort of like to save up for a horse. Then I could go on trail rides, too. Michele wants me to ride with her. She's doing just swell!"

Her mother interrupted from the doorway. "Michele?" she said. "Isn't she that girl you can't stand?"

Darlene felt her face grow hot. "It's different now that I've got to know her." She added shamefacedly, "I guess I never tried to understand her very much."

"Seems to me," her father said, "that there's been some misunderstanding all around. It strikes me now that you'd better take this stable job, since you like it so much."

Darlene rushed at him and hugged him tight. "Oh, Dad, you're out of this world."

Her father held her close. "Well, I think you're pretty great yourself," he said.

Marian Garthwaite

Ana Paula and the Golden Horse

A spent moon huddled over the rancho Ramiriz in the last dark hour of night. The household in the *casa grande* and the Indians in their mud huts slept secure in the peace that brooded, like the moon, over early California and the Spanish missions strung like beads along her coast.

Before the moon was down, Ana Paula heard the sound of her father's voice singing the *alba*. She jumped out of bed and flung back the heavy shutters that barred her deep window. Then her clear soprano joined in the morning hymn to the Virgin.

> "*Ya viene el alba rompiendo el dia*
> *Diganos todos el 'Ave Maria'!*"
>
> "Here comes the dawn breaking
> into the day,
> Let us all sing 'Hail Mary'!"

Ana Paula could hear her mother's voice, and the childish treble of her two younger brothers from their wing of the house across the patio. But not a sound came from Concha's room.

"Slug-a-bed!" scoffed Ana Paula, as she closed her shutters to dress.

Not even on this special day, with the Old One arriving from Monterey any minute for the fiesta of the saint for whom Ana Paula was named, would that lazy Concha get up to greet the morning.

Concha was a thorn in Ana Paula's side. She thought her cousin put on airs, with her grown-up, citified ways, her honey-colored hair, and her wardrobe of latest fashions. Concha never let anyone forget that she was visiting with country cousins—least of all, handsome, young Don Roberto Estodillo.

Yet, for all her languid airs, Concha seemed to manage the household servants easily. And along with the household—Ana Paula's eyes grew stormy as she thought of it—Concha had apparently taken over Don Roberto. *This* was the thorn that festered.

As Ana Paula pulled a fringed buckskin shirt over her head, she was thinking of Roberto. The laughing young don came frequently to the rancho Ramiriz from his father's hacienda in the Salinas valley. He rode often with Ana Paula and her father, Don Felipe. He taught the little boys new tricks of riding and roping at the roundups. Ana Paula had enjoyed his company and taken his friendly ways for granted before Concha came.

Now, instead of accompanying the riders, Roberto loafed about the patio, watching as Concha went prettily about the household tasks with Doña Maria.

Ana Paula's ears burned when she remembered her mother's contented sigh, "At last I have a *daughter* in my home."

Ana Paula considered Concha vain and useless. She herself would much rather ride out at dawn with Don Felipe to rope cattle than stay at home counting linen. Daughter, *vaya!*

It was high noon before Ana Paula saw the cloud of dust moving across the fields where the sea glinted beyond the rocky point.

"Here they come!" she shouted, racing through the patio.

Concha stood in the door of her room, her fair hair pinned high on her head with a shell comb, the ruffles of her dress freshly pressed and crisp.

"Let's ride out to meet them!" urged Ana Paula.

Concha made a little face of distaste. "Would it not be better to welcome Doña Luisa here at the gate?" she suggested.

Ana Paula ran down to the corral where her brothers were waiting for their saddle horses to be cut out from the herd by the vaqueros. "Ask them to rope one for me, too," shouted Ana Paula.

But as soon as their horses were saddled, the boys were off down the road at a hard gallop. It took Ana Paula some time to rope a horse. By the time she had him saddled, she was disheveled and dusty.

"I should have a horse of my own," she grumbled; "one trained to come when I call."

She brushed her arm across her hot face. Her braids were loosened, but with her horse prancing and rearing, she could not spare a hand to rebraid them. Out the gate and down the road she dashed at a headlong gallop.

She met the travelers rounding the curve where the road turned away from the sea. The Old One was riding in a sedan chair that rocked gently on its heavy leather springs between two jogging donkeys. Ana Paula's brothers were riding ahead, Doña Luisa's armed retinue behind.

"Greetings, Godmother," called Ana Paula. "*Amar a Dios!*"

A heavily ringed hand, brown and wrinkled, pushed open the silk curtains; sharp, black eyes peered out, blinking in the sunshine.

Ana Paula was suddenly conscious of her own dusty face, her loosened braids, her long leg, in its fringed legging, draped over the saddle horn.

Her godmother waved wearily and leaned back against the cushions.

Ana Paula's brothers galloped up to her in great excitement.

"Have you seen the palomino?" cried Carlos.

"José is too proud to speak to anyone because he is leading him," added Jaime.

Ana Paula dropped back until she could see the horse José was leading. She drew in her breath in an involuntary gasp of admiration. The animal's golden coat was shining in the sun, his silvery mane and tail blowing in the wind. He was tossing his head, stepping high with pride of breeding. This was an *Ysabella*—a true palomino—the favorite horse of the dons.

Ana Paula's heart began to race with excitement. Could this glorious creature be a present the Old One was bringing to her goddaughter for her name day? Last year her godmother had given Ana Paula pearls from Baja California. Ana Paula knew she would rather have the palomino than anything in the whole, wide world.

Cool and crisp, Concha welcomed them graciously at the gate. The Old One smiled approvingly at her as she climbed out of the sedan chair and groped for her cane.

"Fortunate are the eyes that look upon you,

my child," she murmured, as she kissed Concha on both cheeks.

"Greetings, Godmother," answered Concha. "May you walk with God."

Godmother! Ana Paula had forgotten that the Old One was Concha's godmother as well as her own. Could the palomino be for Concha? The blond horse for the blond girl. There was a bitter olive to chew in that bite.

That afternoon the Old One hobbled out to the corrals. She stood watching as the reata in Ana Paula's hands flew in a lazy curve to coil about the pony Carlos was trying to catch.

The Old One shook her head until her thin gold earrings gleamed in the sunlight.

"It is not good for a girl to be like a rough boy!" she reproved. "Roping horses is men's work. You should be assisting your mother, learning to manage a household. Concha is already a young lady, skilled in household arts."

Ana Paula tightened her rope about a post until Carlos could get a bridle over the horse's head. She flicked the rope loose, coiled it, and tossed it to her brother.

"You are right, *Vieja*," she agreed. "But it seems too bad not to throw a rope when it is so easy for me, and so hard for one so small as Carlos. Having no sons for many years, my father taught me to do these things."

She tucked her hand under the Old One's elbow. "No matter how hard I tried," she added, honestly, "I could never be like Concha."

"A pity!" replied the Old One tartly. "Concha has a way with her."

"Paula is the best roper on the ranch, *Vieja*," Carlos defended his sister with pride. "Father says we could not run a roundup or a matanza without her."

But the Old One was not pleased. "It is a disgrace for your father to allow it. Women should cultivate beauty and charm—not buckskin and ropes!"

Nothing was said about the palomino.

The next day was Ana Paula's name day. This time, when the *alba* was sung, Concha's shutters were wide, and her voice joined in the song of praise.

"Good!" grinned Ana Paula. "All the time the Old One is here, our lazy cousin will have to mend her ways."

She pushed the thought from her as she stood in her window shivering in her long, woolen night robe and doeskin moccasins. The fresh morning air was pouring into the dark little cubby of a room. No unpleasant thoughts, nothing, must spoil this heaven-sent day.

But almost immediately the day turned bitter on Ana Paula's tongue when her godmother handed her an ivory box containing two jade eardrops. The words of thanks came hard.

So the golden horse was for Concha!

After a hasty breakfast of chocolate and *tortillas*, the Ramiriz family and their guests started for the mission. They would hear mass on Ana Paula's name day. Before the sun was above the eastern hills, the long procession was climbing the cliff in the narrow ruts of the old trail.

Don Felipe rode ahead with Doña Maria beside him on a gentle mare. Concha, every curl in place, rode happily between Don Roberto and Don Juanito, who had come up from the Estodillo rancho to join the party. Ana Paula was with Carlos and Jaime, and Doña Luisa's sedan chair came rocking along between the fuzzy donkeys. At the rear rode a small group of vaqueros, but most of the Indians had long since left on foot.

Ana Paula, drinking in the sparkling freshness of the early morning, noticed that Concha kept up a running chatter which, from their laughter, the young men were finding amusing.

Soon they would reach the top of the cliff looking down on the sea. Ana Paula loved this spot where she could almost taste the salt on her lips. She liked to ride along the hard-packed sand just out of reach of the searching scallops of foam. But watching Concha, Ana Paula felt that the morning had suddenly lost its brightness. *La fiesta de mi santo*, she was thinking. The day dedicated to the saint for whom she was named. She was of the age now to be married. It was a frightening thought. She wished she knew the ways to please men, as Concha so evidently did.

They were climbing steadily toward a grove of wind-beaten pines. Suddenly, as they topped the cliff and rounded a bend in the trail, they came upon a huge grizzly bear, feeding on a dead foal at the foot of a tree. Angered at the interruption, the beast stretched to his full height with a roar.

Doña Maria's horse reared and bolted off the trail. Don Felipe, followed by Don Juanito, rode furiously after them, to head them from the cliff's edge. Taken unaware, Concha was thrown from her saddle. Don Roberto's horse was momentarily out of control.

"Lie still, Concha!" shouted Ana Paula, struggling to manage her own horse.

But Concha, screaming, was struggling to her knees, her feet caught in her long riding habit. The grizzly lowered his massive head, his pig eyes gleaming like coals of fire, his jaws slavering blood from his kill.

Ana Paula had been decorously riding side saddle, but now she pulled up her long skirt and swung her leg over the saddle horn. She tore her reata from its fastening. It whistled around her head as she rode toward the bear. For a moment he turned from Concha toward this new menace.

The throw was bad because Ana Paula's horse was plunging and snorting with fear, but the rope settled over the shoulders of the snarling animal. He stopped his lunge to bite and tear savagely at the rope. Don Roberto, his horse now under control, whipped his lariat through the air and caught the bear around the neck.

"Good!" shouted Ana Paula. "Quick! Pull it tight and follow me."

She heard a crash behind her as the sedan chair

tipped over. The Old One rose from between the curtains like a jack-in-the-box. The donkeys were thrashing about between the shafts, blocking the road.

Ana Paula snubbed her rope around the saddle horn. She drove her horse in a wide circle about the pine tree behind the grizzly. Don Roberto followed, his rope choking the bear as he rode. Three times they circled the tree, until the horses could be ridden no closer to the struggling, foaming beast.

Vaqueros rode up. The big bear was now so well trussed up that one of them could approach on foot and kill him.

The ropes were gathered in. The grizzly collapsed in a shaggy heap on the colt he had killed. The sedan chair was righted. The kicking donkeys were quieted. The procession formed again, the trembling Concha in the sedan chair with Doña Luisa. This time Don Roberto was beside Ana Paula.

The sea along which they rode seemed blue and calm after the violence. Later the mission service brought peace and serenity to Ana Paula, kneeling with the women on the hard-packed earthen floor.

After siesta that afternoon, the Old One called Don Roberto to her.

"Will you catch the palomino for me, please?" she asked him.

"*Sí*, Doña Luisa," he answered, "with pleasure."

Followed by the family the Old One stumped out to the gate, pushing the dogs out of her way with her ebony cane.

When Roberto rode up with the palomino there were cries of pleasure.

"What a beauty!"

"A true palomino! See! He is like a king!"

"He is for our horsewoman, Ana Paula," announced the Old One.

Almost speechless with delight, Ana Paula stepped out to receive her gift. The Palomino's golden head was wide between the eyes, with quivering nostrils and sensitive ears. His eyes were dark, and the look he bent on Ana Paula was friendly and intelligent. Ana Paula ran her fingers down his bony muzzle to his velvety lips. He tossed his head until the silver *conchas* on his bridle clinked and jingled.

"*Querida mia!*" murmured Ana Paula, "You darling."

"Could you mean me, Ana Paula?" whispered Don Roberto, as he held his hands together for her to use as a step in mounting.

Ana Paula shook her head, laughing. The color was bright in her brown cheeks, as she placed her foot in his hands and he lifted her to the silver-mounted side saddle.

Then he mounted his own horse and they rode across the fields toward the cliff that looked down on the sea. Not out of sight of the family, for that would never do.

Ana Paula's sun hat was down her back, the ribbons all but choking her. But Don Roberto did not seem to mind. They came galloping back to the gate, laughing together like two children.

At dusk, with the day behind them, Ana Paula was sitting on a stool beside the Old One in her tiny room. A bed of charcoal glowed red in the corner fireplace.

"I cannot thank you enough for the golden horse, *Vieja*," Ana Paula was saying. "He rides like your sedan chair, so easy is his gait. He stands when I saddle him. He seems to enjoy doing what I ask of him. Already we are friends."

"You very nearly didn't get him," the Old One said in her cracked voice. "I had decided to take him back to Monterey with me. I thought you had too many horses for your own good."

Ana Paula stared dreamily into the glowing coals.

"I will try, *Vieja*, to be more of a woman, and less a vaquero."

"You are old enough, now, *niña mia*, to be thinking of marriage."

"I know." Ana Paula's voice was troubled. "My mother never talks of it, but the chests are full to bursting with the quilts and linens." She put her cheek against the wrinkled hand on the old woman's knee. "Oh, *Vieja!* I am not like Concha. I know so little of the ways of men."

The Old One snorted. "You know plenty about roping and riding. The palomino is already eating out of your hand. You'll do. Concha is like the women of Spain. But this is a new world, a new time. Perhaps we Californios need women who can think for themselves when they must."

She stroked Ana Paula's dark head with her old bony fingers.

"There are ways and ways with men, *hija mia*. Who can say which is best?"

Janet Lambert

Tall as the Stars

The small Army post was lazy in the warm fall sunshine. The parade ground, with its surrounding circle of houses, was empty as Judy Roderick scuffled through the dried, rustling leaves on her lawn, tying a limp red ribbon to a stubby yellow pigtail. As she reached her own porch, she gave her hair a last yank—and looked up to see her sister Cynthia looking at her with disapproval.

Cynthia's curls floated loosely on her shoulders, and her eyes, instead of being wide apart and candidly blue, like Judy's, were violets hidden in a deep hedge of lashes. A junior in high school, she was always so intent on her own crowd that she rarely noticed the freshman who was her sister.

Today, however, she put out a hand to stop Judy. "Are you riding in the show tonight?" she asked.

"Sure. Aren't you?"

"I don't know." Her sister's tone was sad, and Judy's eyes opened wide. "I have a terrible problem," Cynthia went on. "Sit down for a minute, will you?"

It was not unusual for Judy to be on the receiving end of a problem, but as it always meant lending Cynthia something, the younger girl was wary. "What's wrong?" she asked. "Charlemagne all right?"

"I suppose so. He's such a stupid goat I don't really care."

"He's a wonderful horse! Dad says—"

"I don't care what Dad says. I'll never get him around the course tonight. I wish I were as good a rider as you are."

Something hammered a warning inside Judy's breast. "You ride fine," she countered quickly. "I bet Charlemagne will win the class."

"He would if *you* rode him. Would you—and let me ride Jack Snipe?"

"No!" Judy flung back her head. "Listen," she said. "You got Charlemagne, when Dad bought us each a horse, because you cried and said you were older. He's lots better than Jack Snipe—or he could be—and you know it. But I've worked hard on Jack, while you just get dressed up and walk along the bridle paths with a lot of boys. If your horse can't win a class it's your fault."

She tried to rise, but Cynthia pulled her back. "Wait a minute!" she wailed. "You don't know how important it is for me to win tonight. If you won't let me ride Jack Snipe—"

"You can just bet I won't!"

"Listen a minute, Judy. You know how I hate history, and how poor my marks have been. This afternoon Mr. MacClendon bawled me out in front of the whole class. He's awfully sarcastic—and when he asked if there was *anything* I was good at, I flared up and said—"

"That you could jump in horse shows," finished Judy.

"Yes. And he looked so amazed that I—well, I guess I laid it on pretty thick, because when I finished telling about the shows and things here at Fort Arden, he said he thought he'd come out to the show tonight!"

"Well, you'll have to make good then," declared Judy.

"I can't—not on Charlemagne! But I know I could win with Jack Snipe."

"Because I've trained him! No. He's my horse and I'm riding him."

Cynthia burst into tears. "I think you're just selfish and mean," she sobbed. "You know Mr. MacClendon will shame me before the whole class."

Judy knew what a build-up Cynthia must have given the horse show—the jumps and the flags, the Army band with its stirring marches. How she must have described the excitement of the general's entrance. And then, because she knew all civilians are interested in the strange world of an Army post, she would have launched into a day at Fort Arden, to lead Mr. MacClendon away from the point of his lecture.

Judy knew how clear the notes of reveille sounded, floating across the early morning air; with what precision the soldiers drilled on the parade ground, marching proudly past under the watchful folds of Old Glory. She loved the sunset gun that stopped the girls and boys on bicycles, the roller skaters, the people in their cars, and held them at attention while the great flag slid slowly down into waiting arms. She loved it all, especially the peaceful sound of taps proclaiming that all was well. And she felt sure that Mr. MacClendon would want to come out to the post to see for himself.

A whistle from a house a short distance away jerked her back to the present, and she turned to see a boy loping across the intervening lawns.

Cynthia dabbed hurriedly at her tears. "I'll just die if you shame me before—"

"Before Bill Hearndon," said Judy grimly. "I get it now. You really want to show off for Bill—not your history teacher."

"Well, sort of. I think he's going to ask me to the Halloween dance. He's wonderful!"

Judy, too, thought Bill was wonderful. He had moved to the post a month ago, and she had discovered how nice he was while she helped him build a pen around his doghouse. Although an upperclassman, Bill never failed to say "Hi, Judy," on the school bus, and sometimes he would stop and talk with her about Jack Snipe.

She had had three whole weeks of enjoying Bill—and now, Cynthia wanted him. Just as she had wanted Judy's best sweater and her gold bracelet, now she wanted Bill Hearndon and Jack Snipe. A depressing wave of futility swept over Judy. When had it ever done her any good to fight against Cynthia?

"Please," Cynthia was whispering. "Oh, please, Judy!"

Judy sighed. After all, a senior wouldn't want to tag around with a freshman forever—not when he could be with Cynthia. So as Bill came up to the porch steps she said, "Oh, all right. Do you want to practice now?"

"Of course not, darling!" Cynthia smiled at Bill. "We're going over to the P. X."

"Want to come along, Jude?" Bill's grin was inviting, but Judy shook her head.

"No, thanks. Guess I'd better see about my tack for tonight."

She watched them cross the parade ground, and then she cut across the tennis courts to the stables. Jack Snipe leaned over the door of his box stall. He was just a brown horse, well bred, with a long, slender neck and intelligent face. As she laid her cheek against his velvet nose, she reached out to pat Charlemagne. He was so beautiful it made one gasp. His registration papers called him a chestnut, but his coat was shining gold, and he had a small white blaze on his forehead, and four dancing white feet.

"Cynthia could have made you a wonder horse," she said as she gave them each a handful of oats.

Then she hunted up a groom. "Please put my saddle on Charlemagne tonight," she told him. "I'm going to ride him."

"Miss Judy!" Private Jones dropped his can of saddle soap. "You've been working so hard with Jack Snipe for that teenagers' class! What's happened? Don't you want to win?"

"Not so very much." She couldn't tell him that she had wanted Bill to see her win with Jack Snipe, nor that Cynthia wanted to ride for him, too. So she only said, "Cynthia's going to ride Jack Snipe tonight. I think she can handle him."

She walked slowly home, and as slowly put on her riding clothes. I didn't have to do it, she thought, as she tied her fractious hair into a pony tail on the back of her neck. Dad would have backed me up.

Judy had always been his favorite. Ever since she was a toddler, following him along the picket line, inspecting the horses and prescribing for their injuries, he had called her Corporal. And as she grew older, his interest in horses had been hers. She had led the horses in and out of their stalls. watering, cleaning, polishing bits and stirrups.

But at dinner that night Colonel Roderick seemed satisfied to accept the change of horses, and listened as Cynthia chattered. Her small chin was pointed above a white stock, and her curls were caught into a net and would make a neat roll under a smart black derby. Judy ate her dinner silently.

But when they were on the way to the riding hall she said earnestly, "Listen, Cee. You think Jack Snipe's a cinch to ride, but he isn't. He can run out like a flash just before a jump, when you can't do a thing."

"I know how to ride," Cynthia laughed. "Just keep your mind on Charlemagne."

The riding hall was already beginning to fill and the tanbark-covered arena was ablaze with lights. Officers and their wives were finding seats in the grandstand at one end, while in an improvised paddock at the other, grooms walked the horses in a circle.

Judy walked through the tanbark, studying the

jumps, figuring how Jack Snipe—not Charlemagne—could weave his way among them.

"You dope," she scolded herself. "You shouldn't want him to win."

As she crawled through the bars of the paddock fence, Cynthia joined her. Jones checked her stirrups and the saddle girth and she began to move Charlemagne around in a circle. She saw that Jack Snipe regarded Cynthia doubtfully, and danced a little when she tried to mount him.

At last the general arrived and the show began. "Teenagers' class," the announcer said through the public-address system. "Eight jumps. Time will be counted in the jump-off in case of a tie. First rider—Richard Compton."

When "Cynthia Roderick" was called, Judy prayed softly, "Please, Jack Snipe, take them all clean for me."

But Jack Snipe was nervous. He had difficulty in lifting himself over the first jump; the second was a double oxer, and he stared at it as if he had never seen one before. But he managed it, and the rest of the jumps, in an awkward performance, straining to free his head.

"You choked him up," Judy scolded when

Cynthia rode in. "You'll never win the jump-off that way."

Her turn was next. Charlemagne was reluctant to exert himself, and she pricked him with her spurs, before she turned him toward the first jump. "Sorry, old fellow," she said. "Steady, now. You can do it."

He took the jump cleanly, and tried so hard on the others that Judy forgot she didn't care about winning, and found herself coaxing, talking, and loving the way his ears came back to listen. He sailed over the last jump with beautiful grace.

"Congratulations!" Bill had been hanging over the wall of the paddock, talking to Cynthia. "Swell going," he went on, grasping Judy's hand. "I'm pulling for you to win."

"Me?" Judy asked. "Why?"

"Because you took a bum horse and gave a whale of a good ride. What made you do it, Judy? Let Cynthia have your horse, I mean?"

"I wanted to."

"Then see it through—and win."

But she turned away from him. "I'll wait to decide," she told herself.

Finally four riders were left to compete in the jump-off: Si Craig, Marty Johnson, Cynthia, and

herself. She sighed as she looked at Cynthia on Jack Snipe. If he won, she could be happy; if he lost, it was no good winning without him.

The starter dropped his red flag and Marty Johnson swung out on the course. His time was good, but Si's was better. Judy, walking Charlemagne in a circle to keep him calm, watched the gate open for Cynthia. Jack Snipe went out like a breeze. He sailed over the jumps. Across the hall, and over. Turn. Over. His head was free, and he forgot that Cynthia was crouched over his neck.

"She's not using a bearing rein," Judy muttered as Jack Snipe thundered along the wall of the riding hall. "She'll have to hold him in." Then she shouted, "Hold him in to the jump, Cynthia!" for Jack Snipe had decided he'd had enough. He shot to the left, by-passed the rails and then whirled around. Cynthia almost went off, but managed to cling ungracefully around his neck, while the gallery applauded.

Then it was Judy's turn. Jack Snipe had lost—should Charlemagne try to win? Loyalty to her own horse, eagerness for Bill's admiration, vied with each other.

Charlemagne took the first jump easily, and

suddenly her decision was made. "I must do what is best for him," she thought. "I must be fair to him." So she helped him at the jumps with encouraging, loving talk, and let him round his turns without pushing him. It was a good ride, but the pleasure was ruined by the black cloud on Cynthia's face when they returned to the paddock.

"I suppose you thought it was funny," she stormed, "to let me ride a quitter."

"He isn't a quitter," Judy hotly defended Jack Snipe. "I warned you to hold him in."

When the announcer called the time that gave her second place, she turned Charlemagne into the ring behind Si. Marty fell in third, and Cynthia brought up the rear. She knew how Cynthia would hate the white fourth-place ribbon she had won.

But Charlemagne arched his neck, when the general's wife hooked the red ribbon on his bridle, as proudly as if it had been the winner's blue. He cantered happily back to the paddock and butted his head against Jones's chest.

"Sure was a pretty ride, Miss Judy," Jones praised.

"Thank you, Jones," she answered. "He's a

sweet horse." She swung her leg over the saddle, then stared down in surprise at Bill.

"Jump!" he ordered. "Let's get some fresh air before we see the rest of the show."

Judy slid down, and let Bill keep her hand as they walked outside.

"There'll be a lot more shows this winter," Bill said. "How about working our horses together, then battling each other for a blue?"

He grinned at her companionably and Judy smiled back. "I'd love to, Bill," she answered a little breathlessly, because her heart was pounding in an odd but happy way.

The sweet notes of Tattoo floated from a bugle on the parade ground. The night air was cool and soft, and Judy looked up at the sky's bright stars. She need only stand on tiptoe to reach up and touch them, she thought.